"Whose baby is it?

Cody demanded.

"You already know the answer."

"I want to hear it from you, Melissa," he snapped. "If I am that child's father, I had a right to know about her when you first discovered you were pregnant."

Melissa met his gaze unflinchingly. "You gave up any rights the day you left town without so much as a goodbye."

"Then the baby really is mine?"

"No doubt about it, at least in anyone's mind except yours."

"Tell me everything about her—what she likes to eat, whether she can talk, how many steps she's taken, if she has allergies, what her favourite toy is..."

Dear Reader:

Romance readers have been enthusiastic about the Silhouette Special Editions® for years. And that's not by accident: Special Editions were the first of their kind and continue to feature realistic stories with heightened romantic tension.

The longer stories, sophisticated style, greater sensual detail and variety that made Special Editions popular are the same elements that will make you want to read book after book.

We hope that you enjoy this Special Edition today, and will enjoy many more.

Please write to us:

Jane Nicholls
Silhouette Books
PO Box 236
Thornton Road
Croydon
Surrey
CR9 3RU

The Cowboy and His Baby

SHERRYL WOODS

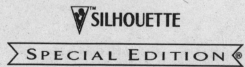

Silhouette, Silhouette Special Edition and Colophon are registered trademarks of Harlequin Books S.A., used under licence.

First published in Great Britain 1997
Silhouette Books, Eton House, 18-24 Paradise Road,
Richmond, Surrey TW9 1SR

© Sherryl Woods 1996

ISBN 0 373 24009 0

23-9702

Printed and bound in Great Britain
by Mackays of Chatham PLC, Chatham

SHERRYL WOODS

lives by the ocean, which, she says, provides daily inspiration for the romance in her soul. She further explains that her years as a television critic taught her about steamy plots and humour; her years as a travel editor took her to exotic locations; and her years as a crummy weekend tennis player taught her to stick with what she enjoyed most—writing. "What better way is there," Sherryl asks, "to combine all that experience than by creating romantic stories?"

Other novels by Sherryl Woods

Silhouette Special Edition®

Safe Harbour
Never Let Go
Edge of Forever
In Too Deep
Miss Liz's Passion
Tea and Destiny
My Dearest Cal
Joshua and the Cowgirl
*Love
*Honour
*Cherish
*Kate's Vow
*A Daring Vow
*A Vow to Love
The Parson's Waiting
One Step Away
Riley's Sleeping Beauty
†A Christmas Blessing
†Natural Born Daddy

†*And Baby Makes Three*
Silhouette Desire®

Not at Eight, Darling
Yesterday's Love
Come Fly with Me
A Gift of Love
Can't Say No
Heartland
One Touch of Moondust
Next Time...Forever
Fever Pitch
Dream Mender

*Silhouette Summer
   Sizzlers 1991*
"A Bridge to Dreams"

*Vows

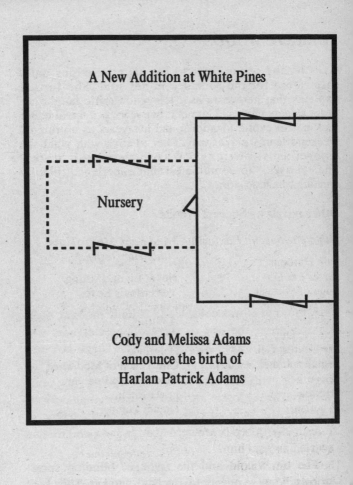

A New Addition at White Pines

Nursery

Cody and Melissa Adams
announce the birth of
Harlan Patrick Adams

Chapter One

Damn, but it was cold, Cody Adams thought as he chased down the last of the herd of cattle he was rounding up. Texas had never been this frigid, not even in the middle of January. He was surprised half the livestock hadn't flat-out frozen in the harsh Wyoming winter. They'd lost a few head of cattle, but nothing like what he'd anticipated the first time the temperatures had dropped below zero and the snow and ice had swirled around him.

The bitter cold and the frequent blinding snowstorms did serve one useful purpose, though. They kept him so busy—kept his brain cells so frozen, for that matter—that he hardly ever thought about home. He'd freeze his butt off and suffer frostbite on most any part of his anatomy for the blessing of a blank memory. He didn't want to think about Texas or his family. Most of all, he didn't want to think about sneaky, conniving Melissa Horton and the way she'd cheated on him.

It had taken him a long time to block out the image of his longtime girlfriend wrapped in his best friend's arms. Even now, more than a year later, that terrible, gut-wrenching moment sneaked up on him when he least expected it and reminded him that that kind of pain might hide out, but it seldom went away.

With the last of the herd rounded up and dusk falling, Cody gestured to one of the other hands that he was leaving and headed back toward the small but cozy line shack he'd insisted he preferred to the bunkhouse. He'd claimed it kept him closer to the cattle for which he was responsible, but the truth was, he craved the isolation.

For a man who had been a very social creature back in Texas—okay, a notorious flirt—it was quite a change and, for the time being, a welcome one. It was the only surefire way he could think of for staying out of trouble and avoiding the sort of heartache that falling for some woman just about guaranteed.

His boss, impressed by the fact that for years 28-year-old Cody had been running White Pines, his family's ranch back in Texas, hadn't argued with his idiosyncratic decision. Lance Treethorn had insisted only that a phone be installed so he could reach Cody on business. He was the only one with the number. He rarely used it. Cody dropped by the ranch house often enough to stay in touch.

On the tiny porch Cody stomped the snow off his boots, gathered up an armload of firewood and went inside. Within minutes he had a fire roaring and had shucked off his skeepskin jacket. He stood in front of the blaze, letting the heat warm his chilled body. Unfortunately, it couldn't touch the cold place deep inside him.

He'd been standing there for some time, lost in thought, when he noticed the stack of mail sitting on the table in the kitchen area of the one-room cabin. It was sitting atop a foil-covered pan that he suspected from the sinful, chocolaty aroma, contained a batch of freshly baked brownies. He grinned and ripped off the foil. Sure enough, brownies. Apparently, Janey Treethorn had been by again.

The fifteen-year-old daughter of his boss had a giant-size crush on him. Thankfully, though, she was painfully shy. She limited her overtures to dropping off his mail, always with a batch of brownies or his favorite apple pie. In the summer it had been fresh fruit cobblers. She was usually careful to stop by while he wasn't home. On the one occasion when he'd caught her, she'd blushed furiously, stammered an apology for intruding, and fled on horseback before he could even say thanks.

Unable to resist, he grabbed one of the brownies and ate it as he sorted through the few pieces of mail she'd left, putting the bills aside to be paid later. A small blue envelope caught his attention. Turning it over, he recognized his sister-in-law's handwriting.

As always, when anything came from a member of his family, his heart skipped a beat. Letters were rare enough to stir a pang of homesickness each time one arrived. Jordan's wife had been dutifully writing to him once every two weeks or so from the moment she and Jordan had gotten married. For a man who swore he wanted nothing to do with anyone or anything back home, it was downright pitiful how he looked forward to Kelly's chatty letters and the family gossip she shared with such humor and telling insight. This one was more than a week overdue. Since the others had come like clockwork, he'd been trying not to admit just how worried he really was.

He could tell right off there was something different about this one, too. It was stiffer, more like a card than a letter. He grabbed a second brownie, then carried Kelly's latest correspondence with him back to his chair in front of the fire.

When he ripped open the envelope, a tiny square dropped out of the card inside. He grabbed for it instinctively and found himself staring at an infant swaddled as tight as a papoose in a blue blanket. He caught himself grinning at the sight of that tiny, red, scrunched-up face.

So, Jordan was a daddy, he thought, amazed by the shaft of pure envy that shot through him. He'd known the baby was due any day now. Kelly had kept him apprised of every detail of her pregnancy, including his older brother's bemusement at the natural childbirth classes she'd insisted he take with her. He wondered if

Jordan had made it through the delivery or if he'd fainted at Kelly's first big-time contraction.

He closed his eyes against the tide of longing that rolled over him. He was missing so damned much, he thought, once again cursing Melissa for the betrayal that had made staying in Texas where he belonged impossible.

He was missing seeing his other brother Luke and his wife Jessie's little girl grow. Angela had turned two back in December. Kelly had sent a picture of her with her face streaked with icing and her fist in the middle of the chocolate birthday cake with its two, fat pink candles. He'd tucked it in his wallet, along with the snapshot of Kelly's daughter from her first marriage, Dani, a little con-artist-in-training who could persuade penguins to buy ice, if she was of a mind to. Now he opened his wallet and inserted the tiny picture of this latest addition to the family.

He stared at the brand new baby one last time and wondered if he'd ever see him. He'd been named Justin James, according to the information on the birth announcement.

"We're going to call him J.J.," Kelly wrote in the note accompanying the card. "We can't wait for you to see him. Jordan swears he hasn't slept a wink in the past week. I don't know how that can be, since I'm the one up every time the little monster screams in the middle of the night. I haven't noticed Jordan pacing the floor alongside me. I think he's been sleeping with a pillow over his head deliberately, so he can claim he never hears J.J. crying. He swears he only wakes up after I've already left the bed. The silver-tongued devil says it's missing me that wakes him. He thinks a line like that will make me more sympathetic to him. Fat chance.

"No, seriously," he read on, "your big brother has been a huge help. I think he's a little awed by father-hood...or maybe it's just that mountain of diapers he's expected to wash every night."

Cody chuckled at the image of his button-down brother, the big-time oil company executive, changing diapers and warming bottles. Maybe he was taking to it better than any of them had anticipated, including Jordan himself.

"We're scheduling the baptism for the end of the month and we expect you to be here," the letter continued. "No excuses, Cody. It's time to come home."

It's time to come home. Kelly's words echoed in his head, taunting him, reminding him that nothing would ever make this beautiful, sprawling Wyoming ranch into home. Lance Treethorn was a kind, decent man. He'd become a good friend. His daughters were real little angels and they treated Cody like one of the family. Even so, it wasn't the same. Not that a little thing like being homesick mattered. Even though his heart ached for the life he'd left behind, he knew he could never go back. He'd rather eat dirt than get within a hundred miles of the traitorous Melissa ever again.

It had been over a year since he'd left Texas, eighteen months to be exact, but not even time had cured him of the rage that had sent him away from everyone and everything dear to him.

Mention Texas and he didn't think of his beloved White Pines, didn't think of his parents or his brothers, much as he loved them all. The only image that inevitably came to mind was of Melissa Horton. Sometimes not even an entire bottle of the best liquor in the store could blot out the memories of the woman who'd betrayed him with his best friend.

Even now the vision in his head of Melissa was so vivid he could practically feel the silky texture of her skin and the soft flow of dark auburn hair through his fingers. He could practically smell the sweet summer scent of her.

But along with the sensual memories came the blinding rage, as powerful now as it had been on the day he'd left Texas for good. Accompanying that rage was the anger and frustration of realizing that he was, in part, responsible for what had happened. Maybe if he'd told her he loved her, she wouldn't have turned to Brian Kincaid in the first place. Maybe if he'd had a clue just how much she mattered to him, instead of taking her for granted, he wouldn't be lying awake nights aching for her. He'd been a fool. She'd been a cheat. Quite a pair, the two of them. Maybe he deserved to be this miserable. She certainly did, though he had no idea if she was. She could be happily married to Brian now, for all he knew.

Before he'd realized what he was doing, he'd ripped the note inviting him to the baptism of Jordan and Kelly's baby to shreds. He couldn't allow himself to be tempted back, not even by something as important as this. He would not go back to Texas. Not now. Not ever.

The decision was firm, but it left him feeling heart-sick and more lonely than he'd ever felt in his life. He was almost glad when the ring of the phone shattered the silence. He grabbed the receiver gratefully.

"Hey, boss, what's up?" he said, knowing it would be Lance Treethorn on the other end of the line.

The widowed father of three young girls, Treethorn had his hands full with trying to run the ranch and raise his daughters to be proper young ladies. He'd suc-ceeded with the oldest. Janey was as prim and proper and dutiful as a father could ever want, but the two younger ones, ten and twelve, were terrors. Cody didn't envy the thirty-five-year-old man trying to get them raised and married without calamity striking.

"We got the herd rounded up today," he told Lance. "We only lost one more to the cold."

"Thanks, Cody, but I didn't call for an update."

Something in Lance's voice triggered alarm bells. "What's wrong?" he asked at once. "Are there prob-lems with the girls?"

"No, it's nothing like that. We're all fine, but you had a call here at the house."

"I did?" He'd given the Treethorn number only to Jordan, with a direct order that it never be used except for a dire emergency. He knew his brother would never break that rule. His heart thudded dully as he waited for whatever bad news Jordan had imparted.

"Call home," his boss told him. "It sounded pretty urgent. Your brother asked how quickly I could get a message to you. Obviously Jordan still doesn't know you have a phone in your cabin."

"No," Cody admitted, grateful that his boss had never asked why he insisted on having such a buffer between him and his family. Lance was the best kind of boss, the best kind of friend. He was scrupulously fair. He lent support, but never asked questions or made judgments. There had been no hint of criticism in his voice when he'd commented just now on Cody's decision to keep his private phone number from his family.

"I'm sorry he bothered you," Cody apologized anyway.

"You know damned well it's no bother. I just hope everything's okay at home. Give me a call if there's anything I can do to help."

"Thanks, Lance."

Cody hung up slowly, thinking of the tiny picture that he'd placed in his wallet only moments earlier. Had something happened to Justin James? Or to Kelly? Why else would Jordan call? Damn, but he hated being so far away. What if... He allowed the thought to trail off.

"Stop imagining the worst and call," he muttered out loud, finally forcing himself to dial his brother's number, knowing that this call, whatever it was about, would shatter whatever distance he'd managed to achieve from his past.

Jordan picked up on the first ring. His voice sounded tired and hoarse.

"Hey, big brother," Cody said.

"Cody, thank God. I was worried sick you wouldn't get the message for days."

Jordan, the most composed man Cody had ever known, sounded shaken. The alarm bells triggered by Lance's call were clanging even louder now. "What's wrong?"

"It's bad news, Cody. Real bad."

Cody sank onto a chair by the kitchen table and braced himself. The last time Jordan had sounded that somber was when their brother Erik had been killed in an accident on Luke's ranch.

"Is it Dad?" he asked, hating even to form the words. Harlan Adams was bigger than life. He was immortal—or so Cody had always tried to tell himself. He couldn't imagine a world in which Harlan wasn't controlling and manipulating things.

"No, he's fine," Jordan reassured him at once, then amended, "Or at least as well as can be expected under the circumstances."

"Dammit, Jordan, spit it out. What the hell has happened?"

"It's Mother," he began, then stopped. He swallowed audibly before adding, "She and Daddy were out riding this morning."

He paused again and this time Cody could hear his ragged breathing. It almost sounded as if Jordan were crying, but that couldn't be. Jordan never cried. None of them did. Harlan had very old-fashioned ideas on the subject of men and tears. He had set a tough example for them, too. He hadn't shed a single tear when Erik died. He'd just retreated into stony, guilt-ridden silence for months after the loss of his son. The rest of them had coped with their grief dry-eyed, as well. If Erik's death hadn't caused Jordan's cool, macho facade to crack, what on earth had?

"Jordan, are you okay?" he asked.

"No. Mother took a bad fall, Cody."

Cody felt as if the blood had drained out of him. Hands trembling, he grabbed the edge of the table and held on. "How is she? Is she . . ."

"She's gone, Cody," Jordan said with a catch in his voice. "She never woke up. She was dead by the time the paramedics got to the ranch."

"My God," he murmured, stunned. Forbidden tears stung his eyes. Ashamed, he wiped at them uselessly. They kept coming, accompanied by a terrible sense of loss. "Are you sure Daddy's okay? Why aren't you with him?"

"Luke and Jessie are over at White Pines now. Luke's got the funeral arrangements under control. Kelly and I will be going over right after I get off the phone. I wanted to stay here until you called back. How soon can you get here?"

Cody noticed his brother asked the question as if there were no doubt at all that he would be coming home. "I don't know," he said, struggling between duty and the agony that going home promised.

Disapproving silence greeted the reply. "But you will be here," Jordan said emphatically. "I'm telling Daddy you're on your way."

Cody rubbed his suddenly pounding head. "I don't know," he repeated.

"Look, this is no time to be indulging in self-pity, little brother," Jordan snapped impatiently. "Daddy needs you here, probably more than he needs any of the rest of us. He'll need you to take up some of the slack at White Pines while he pulls himself together. He's always depended on you. Don't let him down now."

Cody said nothing.

Jordan finally broke the silence with a sigh. "We're scheduling the funeral for Saturday," he said. "Be here, Cody."

He hung up before Cody could reply.

Cody sat in the gathering darkness, silent, unchecked tears streaking down his cheeks. He had no choice and he knew it. Mary Adams might not have been the kind of warm, doting mother a child dreamed of, but Harlan Adams had worshiped her. He could not let his father go through this kind of grief without all of his sons at his side. It was the kind of loyalty that had been ingrained in him since birth. As badly as he wanted to pretend it didn't matter, he knew better. Nothing mattered more at a time like this.

He took some small comfort in the odds that said he would probably never even see Melissa. He doubted she would have the nerve to show up at the funeral. She certainly wouldn't have the audacity to show up at White Pines afterward. It would be okay. He could slip in and out of town before temptation overtook him and he sought out so much as a glimpse of her.

At least, that's what he told himself on the long, sad drive back to Texas after he'd cleared his departure with Lance. He'd chosen to drive to delay his arrival as long as possible. Maybe to come to grips with what had happened in private. He'd spend a few days with his family to grieve. A few days to do whatever he could for his father. A few days to spoil his nieces and hold his brand new nephew. A few days to soak up enough memories to last a lifetime.

With all that going on, Melissa would be the last thing on his mind.

The very last thing, he vowed with grim determination as he finally turned into the lane to White Pines.

He slowed his pickup and looked around at the land that he loved, the land he'd hoped one day would be his since Luke's mile-wide independent streak had sent him chasing after his own dream and his own ranch and Jordan was only interested in oil.

Even in the dead of winter, it was starkly beautiful, at least to him. He was home and suddenly, despite the sorrow that had drawn him back, he felt at peace for the first time since he'd driven away more than eighteen months before.

Melissa Horton took a break from her job behind the lunch counter at Dolan's Drugstore and perched on a stool with the weekly newspaper and a cup of coffee. Her attention was riveted to the story of Mary Adams's tragic riding accident.

The 55-year-old woman had always been incredibly kind to her. Melissa had figured Mary pitied her because she'd been mooning around Cody for most of her life. Once Mary had even tried to give her some advice. It had turned out to be lousy advice, but Melissa was certain Mary had thought she was doing her a favor.

Mary had sat her down one afternoon over tea and told her that Cody was taking her for granted. Not that that was news. At any rate, Mary had claimed that the only way Melissa would ever win him would be to make him jealous. Tired of being ignored except when it suited Cody, and taking the well-meant advice to heart, Melissa had tried to do just that by going out just once with Cody's best friend.

What a disaster that had been! Had she chosen anyone else, maybe the plan would have worked, but she'd foolishly selected the one man she'd figured wouldn't get hurt. Brian had known her heart belonged to Cody. He'd known their date meant nothing, that it was only a ploy to shake up Cody. He'd even tried to argue her out of it, warning her it could backfire, but her mind had been made up. She had risked everything, certain that Mary Adams was right. She'd seen it as the only way to get Cody to finally make a commitment to her.

She should have guessed that Brian understood Cody even better than she did. Every time she thought of the anger and hurt in Cody's eyes that night, it made her sick to her stomach. He had stared at them for the space of one dull, thudding heartbeat. He'd looked not at her, but through her. His gaze riveted on Brian, he'd said, "A hell of a friend you turned out to be."

He had spoken with a kind of lethal calm that had been more chilling than shouted accusations. Then he'd turned on his heel and walked away. He had taken off the next morning and never once looked back.

For the past eighteen months she'd had no idea at all where he was. Brian hadn't heard from him, hadn't expected to, for that matter. She hadn't had the courage to ask Cody's family for information. Her shame ran too deep.

There had been times when she'd considered being in the dark a blessing. It had kept her from chasing after him, from destroying what few shreds of pride and dignity she had left.

Now, though, she had no doubts at all that Cody would be coming home. She might have driven him away with her betrayal, but his mother's death would surely bring him back.

Had he changed much? she wondered. Had he lost the flirtatious, fun-loving nature that had charmed her and half the women who'd crossed his path? Would she have to live with regrets for the rest of her life for turning him into a bitter, cynical man?

"No good'll come of what you're thinking," Mabel Hastings advised, coming up behind her to peer over her shoulder at the front page of the newspaper.

"How do you know what I'm thinking?" Melissa asked defensively.

Mabel shook her head, her tight gray curls bouncing at the movement. When Mabel had a permanent, she meant it to last. She'd been wearing the exact same hairstyle as far back as Melissa could remember. It did not suit her pinched features.

"I been reading you like a book ever since you set eyes on Cody Adams way back in junior high school," Mabel informed her huffily. "You seem to forget how many times you sat right here at this very counter making goo-goo eyes at him."

Melissa chuckled despite her irritation at the unsolicited interference. "'Goo-goo eyes'? Mabel, exactly how old are you? A hundred, maybe? Not even my mother would use an expression like that."

The older woman, who was probably no more than sixty, scowled at her. "Don't matter what you call it, the point is you've been crazy about that boy way too long and just look where it got you."

Melissa sensed the start of a familiar lecture. Listening to it was the price she paid for having a job that paid enough in salary and tips to keep her financially afloat and independent. She didn't have to take a dime from her parents.

"Okay, I get your point," she said, trying to avoid the full-scale assault on her sense and her virtue. "Drop it, please. I probably won't even see Cody."

She was bright enough to know it would be far better if she didn't. Her life had taken some unexpected twists and turns since he'd left, but it was settling down now. She was at peace with herself. There were no more complications, no more tears in the middle of the night over a man who didn't love her—at least, not enough—and no more roller coaster ups and downs.

No way did she want to stir up old memories and old hurts. One look into Cody's laughing brown eyes and she couldn't trust herself not to tumble straight back into love with him. She'd clearly never had a lick of sense where he was concerned.

Now, though, the stakes were way too high. Now she had more than her own heart to consider. She had someone else to protect, someone more important to her than life itself—Cody's daughter, the child he didn't even know he had.

Chapter Two

The entire family was walking around in a daze. Cody had never seen them like this, not even when Erik died. He supposed they were all following Harlan's lead. His father hadn't spoken more than a word or two to anyone. He hadn't eaten. He wasn't sleeping. He had refused a sedative prescribed by the doctor. Not even his unusually subdued grandchildren, tugging on his sleeves and competing for his attention, drew so much as a smile. He looked haggard and lost.

On Saturday morning Cody found Harlan in his office, staring at nothing, his complexion a worrisome shade of gray. Cody walked over and perched on a corner of his desk.

"Hey, Daddy, are you doing okay?"

Harlan blinked, his gaze finally focusing. "Cody, have you been here long?"

The vague question startled Cody. Normally nothing went on at White Pines that Harlan didn't notice. "Actually, I got here yesterday."

His father's lips quirked for a fraction of a second. "Hell, I know that. I haven't lost my marbles. I meant now. Have you been standing there long?"

Relief sighed through Cody. "Nope. Just walked in. Everyone's been looking for you."

"Must not have been looking too hard," Harlan grumbled in a manner that was more in character. "I've been right here all night long."

Cody was dismayed. "You didn't sleep?"

"Off and on, I suppose."

"Daddy, you should have been resting. Today's going to be rough enough without facing it exhausted."

His father shrugged. "I couldn't go upstairs."

"Damn," Cody muttered. Why hadn't any of them thought of that? Of course it was going to be hard for their father to spend time in the suite of rooms he had shared for so many years with his wife. It was hard for the rest of them just being in the house where their mother had reigned over every last detail. "I'm sorry. I'll go upstairs and bring some clothes down for you. It'll be time to go to the church soon."

He had barely reached the door when his father's voice stopped him.

"How could a thing like this happen?" Harlan murmured.

His choked voice sounded too damned close to tears. Cody was shaken by that as he hadn't been by anything else in his life.

"We were supposed to have so many years left," Harlan went on. "I had promised your mother we'd travel, that we'd see all the sights she'd been reading about over the years." He glanced at Cody. "Did you know she gave up a trip around the world for her college graduation to marry me? I promised to make it up to her one day, but I never got around to it."

Guilt sliced through Cody. His departure had kept them from going on those trips. His father had had to take over the running of White Pines again, just when he'd been ready to indulge all of his wife's fantasies.

"You can't think about that," Cody told him, partly because he couldn't bear to think about it, either. "You'll make yourself crazy. Think about the years you did have. You made Mother very happy. She loved being your wife. She loved being mistress of White Pines. She was wild about all those fancy ancestors of yours."

"She loved you boys, too," Harlan added quietly. "Oh, I know she didn't pay you the kind of attention she did me. I regret that. I regret that you all thought that meant she didn't love you."

At Cody's expression of shock, he added, "Don't deny it, son. I know you boys couldn't help feeling that way. Catering to me was just your mama's way. When you were little, I don't think she knew quite what to make of you. She was an only child. She wasn't prepared for the chaos of four rambunctious boys. But she cared about you and she was so very proud of the way you all turned out.''

''Even me?'' Cody asked, unable to prevent the question from popping out. He hated what it said about his insecurities. He had feared that turning his back on White Pines would cost him whatever affection either of his parents felt for him.

Harlan chuckled. ''Are you kidding? You were her baby. There wasn't a day since you've been gone that she didn't worry about you and how you were getting along, when she didn't tell me how she missed hearing you thundering down the stairs or raising a ruckus in the kitchen.''

''She hated it when I did those things,'' Cody protested.

''Only until they stopped,'' Harlan said softly. Sorrow had etched new lines in his face. The sadness behind the comment emphasized them.

Cody watched with amazement and new respect as his father visibly pulled himself up, gathering strength from some inner reserve that had been severely tested in the past few days. He stood, crossed the room and put a comforting arm around Cody's shoulders, sharing that strength with his son.

''Come on, boy. Help me figure out what to wear, so I won't put your mama to shame.''

Together they climbed the stairs and went to prepare for the funeral of the woman Cody had adored and on occasion admired, but until just this morning had never understood.

* * *

Melissa watched the clock above the soda fountain ticking slowly toward noon. She would not go to Mary's funeral. She would not! If she did, she would be going for all the wrong reasons.

Drugstore owner and pharmacist Eli Dolan came out from behind the prescription counter, then peered at her over the rim of his reading glasses. "You going?"

"Going where?" Melissa asked.

He muttered something about women and foolishness under his breath. "To that funeral, of course. You ought to be paying your respects."

She didn't bother asking how Eli knew that she had been close to Mary at one time. Everyone in town knew everyone else's business. That's what had made staying here after her daughter was born so difficult. She doubted there was a single soul that didn't have their suspicions about the identity of Sharon Lynn's daddy, but as far as she knew only her own parents and Cody's brother Jordan and his wife knew the truth for certain.

She wouldn't have admitted it to Jordan and Kelly, but he had taken one look at the baby and guessed. She hadn't been able to deny it. Jordan had vowed to keep her secret and, as far as she knew, he'd been true to his word. She was ninety-eight percent certain that he'd never told Cody. Harlan had instilled a deep sense of honor in all of his sons. That included keeping promises, even when extracted under the most trying conditions.

She also had a hunch that if Jordan had told, Cody would have stormed back to Texas and raised a commotion that would have set the whole town on its ear. Or maybe that was just wishful thinking on her part.

"You'd better get a move on, if you're going to find a place in church," Eli prompted, clearly not intending to let the matter drop. "It's bound to be crowded. Folks around here think mighty highly of Harlan and his sons. They'll be there for them, even if most of them found Mary a little high-falutin' for their taste."

"I can't leave here now," Melissa hedged, taking another wipe at the already polished counter. "It's lunchtime."

"And who's going to be here?" he shot right back. "Everybody will be at the funeral. I don't expect we'll be doing much business. And you seem to forget that I was making milk shakes and sandwiches when you were still in diapers. I can handle things for the next couple of hours. If I make a mess of things, you can say you told me so when you get back."

He glanced over at Mabel and nodded in her direction. "Or she'll do it for you," he said with a sour note in his voice. "Now, go on. Do what you know is right."

Melissa didn't question the sense of relief she felt at being nudged determinedly out the door. If Eli didn't find it odd that she'd be going to the funeral, maybe no one else would, either. Maybe it would have been more noticeable if she'd stayed away.

Bracing herself against the brisk January wind, she rushed down Main Street, glad that she'd chosen to wear a dress to work rather than her usual jeans and

T-shirt. Obviously some part of her had known even when she'd dressed that morning that she would change her mind about going to the service.

It was a dreary day for a funeral. Leaden clouds, practically bursting with rain—or, given the rapidly dropping temperature, more likely sleet—hung low in the sky. She tugged her coat more tightly around her, but gave up on keeping her long hair from tangling as the wind whipped it around her face.

All the way to the church she tried to keep her mind off Cody and on the service that was to come. Her best efforts, however, were a dismal failure. She kept envisioning Cody, wondering how he was holding up, worrying how he and all of his brothers were doing and regretting more than she could say that she couldn't take her place with them and offer the support she desperately wanted to give.

She was so late that she planned to slip into the back of the church and stand in the shadows. Cody would never know she was there. The last thing she wanted to do today was add to his misery.

She ran up the steps of the old church just as the bells were chiming in the tall white steeple. The sun peeked through the clouds for just an instant, creating a terrible glare. Going from that sudden bright sun outside into the church's dimly lit interior, she was momentarily blinded.

Apparently, whoever was hard on her heels was having the same problem because he slammed smack into her, his body rock solid as he hit her at full tilt. The contact almost sent her sprawling on the polished wood floor.

"Sorry," he said, gripping her elbows to keep her upright. "You okay, darlin'?"

Melissa's heart climbed straight into her throat. She would have recognized that voice, that automatic flirtatiousness, even if she hadn't heard it for a hundred years. The firm, steadying touch was equally familiar and just as devastating. If she'd brushed against a live wire, she couldn't have felt any more electrified.

"Cody?"

She spoke his name in no more than a whisper, but at the sound of her voice, he jerked his hands away as if he'd just touched a white-hot flame.

"Excuse me," he said, his voice instantly like ice.

As if she were a stranger, he shoved past her to make his way to the front of the church. No, she corrected, if she'd been a stranger, he would have been less rude, more solicitous.

Trembling from the unexpected face-to-face meeting, Melissa watched him stride up the aisle to join his father and his brothers in the first pew. In that single quick glimpse, she had seen new lines in his face. His sun-streaked, normally untamed hair had been trimmed neatly in the way his mother had always wanted it to be.

It was his eyes, though, that had stunned her. Once they'd been filled with so much laughter. Naturally she had expected to find sorrow today in the dark-as-coffee depths. What she hadn't anticipated was the cold an-

tipathy when he recognized her, followed by an emp-
tiness that was worse than hatred.

Well, she thought despondently, now she knew.
Cody hadn't forgiven her. He'd looked straight
through her as if he'd never known her, as if he'd never
teased her or made love to her or shared his deepest,
darkest secrets with her.

"Oh, God," she murmured in what could have been
the beginning of a prayer, but instead simply died before completion. Their relationship was clearly beyond even divine intervention. She'd known it all
along, of course, but she hadn't wanted to believe it.
The last flicker of hope in her heart died like a candle
flame in a chilly wind.

Though a part of her wanted to flee, she moved into
the deepest shadows and stayed through the service,
grieving not just for the woman lying in the flower-
draped casket, but for the death of her own dreams.

"You went to the funeral, didn't you?" Velma Horton asked the minute Melissa walked through her
mother's doorway to pick up her daughter after work.

"How did you know?" she asked, though it was easy
enough to guess. The grapevine had probably been
buzzing all afternoon and her mother was definitely
tapped into that.

Her mother sniffed. "You think I didn't know why
you wore that dress today. I know what you said, some
nonsense about all your jeans being in the laundry, but
I'm not a fool, girl. I knew you wouldn't miss a chance
to catch sight of Cody. So, did you see him?"

"Briefly," Melissa admitted.

"And?"

"And what? We didn't talk."

"Then you didn't tell him about Sharon Lynn."

Melissa shook her head. "He wouldn't care," she said with absolute certainty that was based on the way he'd looked straight through her for the second time in their lives.

To her surprise, her mother breathed a sigh of relief and some of the tension drained out of her expression. "Good."

There were times, like now, when Melissa didn't understand her mother at all. When Velma had learned her daughter was pregnant, she'd been all for chasing Cody to the ends of the earth and demanding he take responsibility for his actions.

"I thought you wanted him to know," Melissa said, regarding her mother with confusion. "There was a time you threatened to go to Harlan and demand that he drag Cody back here. You thought he owed me his name and his money. The only thing that stopped you was Daddy's threat to divorce you if you did."

Velma rolled her eyes. "Your father's got more pride than sense. Anyway, that was before Sharon Lynn was born, back when I didn't know how you'd manage by yourself. Seems to me you've done just fine. There's no sense in trying to fix what's not broke."

It was a reasonable explanation for the turnaround, but Melissa didn't entirely buy it. "There's something else, isn't there? Some other reason you don't want Cody to find out the truth?"

"There is," her mother admitted, an ominous note in her voice. "Harlan Adams is a powerful man."

"That's not news. What's your point? What does he have to do with this? It's between me and Cody."

"Not if Harlan gets it into his head to claim his granddaughter," her mother stated, a note of genuine fear in her voice. "There's no way we could fight a man like that."

Melissa was stunned by what her mother was suggesting. "Don't you think you're being a little paranoid? Jordan's known for almost a year now and he hasn't even spilled the beans. I suspect the rest of the family will react with just as much indifference."

Her mother didn't seem to be reassured. "Just watch your step. I'm warning you, Melissa, keep that baby as far away from Cody Adams as you can."

Though she didn't think the warning was necessary, Melissa nodded dutifully. "I don't think we have to worry about that. Cody will probably be gone before we know it."

Just then the sounds of her daughter's cheerful, nonsensical babbling echoed down the narrow hallway. Melissa smiled. Her heart suddenly felt lighter than it had all day. The baby had had that effect on her from the moment she'd been born.

"Did she just wake up?" she asked as she started toward her old bedroom.

"I doubt she's even been asleep. She didn't want to go down for her nap. I think she sensed the tension in both of us. You go on in. I'm going to fix your daddy's dinner."

Melissa went to pick up her daughter from the crib her mother had put up next to the twin bed Melissa had slept in for most of her life. Sharon Lynn was standing on shaky, pudgy little legs, hanging on to the crib rail. Her eyes lit up when she spotted her mother.

"Ma...ma...ma."

"That's right, darling girl," Melissa crooned, gathering her into her arms. "I'm your mama."

She inhaled the sweet talcum-powder scent of her baby and sighed as tiny little hands grabbed her hair and held on tight. "You've got quite a grip, little one. You must have gotten that from your daddy. I'm the original hundred-pound weakling."

"Da?" Sharon Lynn repeated, echoing a sound Melissa had taught her while showing her a snapshot of Cody. Her mother would have pitched a royal fit if she'd known.

"Oh, baby," she murmured, tightening her embrace. "Your daddy's right here in town. He has no idea what he's been missing all these months. He has no idea that he has a precious little girl."

Cody would have made a wonderful father, she thought with a sigh. He would have been too indulgent by far, too readily conned by sweet talk and a winning smile, but, oh, how he would have cherished and protected a child of his. Her foolish actions had cost him the chance to prove that. Worse, they had cost her daughter a chance to be loved by an incredible man. There were days when she almost made herself sick with regrets.

"We do okay by ourselves, though, don't we?" she asked, gazing into round, dark eyes that reminded her too much of Cody. The baby returned her gaze with the kind of serious, thoughtful look the question deserved. Melissa wondered how many years it would be before that innocent contemplation turned to something far more accusatory because her mother had robbed her of any contact with her father.

"Don't," her mother pleaded, coming up behind her.

"Don't what?"

"Don't tell him."

"Who said I was going to?" Melissa asked.

"I know that look. You're making up pipe dreams about what it will be like when Cody finds out he has a baby girl. You're expecting him to declare he's never stopped loving you and sweep you off to get married."

Her expression turned dire. "It won't be that way, I'm telling you. If he cares about the baby at all, he'll take her from you. That's how much he hates you for what you did to him. You made a fool of him in front of the whole town by going out with his best friend. A man never forgets a betrayal like that. I don't care if it was just a bunch of foolishness on your part. The results were the same as if you and Brian had had something going."

"You don't know anything about Cody's feelings," Melissa argued, even though she had just seen with her own eyes that Cody did despise her. She didn't want to believe he could be cruel enough to try to take their daughter away from her.

"Are you willing to take that chance?" her mother demanded.

The baby whimpered, either because she was picking up on the sudden tension or because Melissa was holding her too tightly. "No," she whispered, fighting the sting of tears as she kissed her daughter's silky cheek. "No, I'm not willing to take that chance."

She had been weaving pipe dreams, just as her mother had guessed. The risk of trying to make them come true, though, was far too great. Rather than winning back Cody, she could very well lose her child. She would die before she let that happen. Sharon Lynn was the most important thing in her life.

All the way home she assured herself that she only needed a few days. If she kept the secret just a few more days, Cody would be gone and that would be the end of it.

Later that night she sank into the rocker beside Sharon Lynn's crib and set it into motion, hoping to lull the baby to sleep and to quiet all those clamoring shouts in her head that told her she just might be making the second worst mistake in her life by keeping silent. As much as she hated to admit it, her mother was right about one thing. If Cody did learn the truth from someone else, there was no telling what he might do to exact revenge.

Chapter Three

For the past two days Cody hadn't been able to stop thinking about his brief meeting with Melissa at the funeral. She looked exactly as he'd remembered her, her long hair a tangle of fiery lights, her body slender as a reed except for the lush, unexpected curve of her breasts.

Even before he'd heard her voice, in that instant when he'd caught her to prevent her from falling, he'd known it was her just from the way his body had reacted to touching her. He had hated that reaction, hated knowing that his desire for her hadn't waned at all despite the months of self-imposed exile. That seemed like the cruelest sort of punishment.

Late that night after the funeral he'd been pacing downstairs when his father had come out of his office and caught him. Harlan had guessed right off that his agitation had to do with Melissa, though he'd been uncommonly cautious in broaching the subject.

"I thought I saw Melissa at the church today," Harlan had said casually after he'd pulled Cody into his office and they were both seated in comfortable leather chairs in front of a blazing fire, glasses of whiskey in hand. At the reference to Melissa, Cody had put his aside without tasting it. He'd feared if he got started, he'd never stop.

"She was there," he'd conceded, his voice tight.

"Did you get a chance to talk to her?"

"We have nothing to say to each other."

"I see," Harlan said. He'd let the silence build for a bit, taking a sip of his drink before adding nonchalantly, "I heard she's been working at Dolan's Drugstore, running the soda fountain for Eli. Doing a good job, too. Eli says business is up. The kids are hanging out there again instead of driving to the fast-food place out on the highway."

Cody hadn't even acknowledged the information. He'd just tucked it away for later consideration. Ever since, he'd been considering what to do about it.

He could drive into town, march into Dolan's and confront Melissa about what she'd done to him, something he probably should have done the very night he'd found her with Brian. He could raise the kind of ruckus that would be the talk of the town for the next year. It would go into the textbook of Cody Adams lore that had begun when he was barely into puberty.

If half the tales had been true, he would have worn himself out by the time he was twenty.

Sighing, he conceded he couldn't see much point to adding another wild exploit to his reputation. A scene would only rake up old news, embarrass Melissa—not that he cared much about that—and tell anyone with half a brain that Cody wasn't over her. Otherwise, why would he bother to stir up the cold ashes of their very dead relationship?

No, for the sake of his own pride if nothing else, it was better to stay the hell away from town. He repeated the advice to himself like a mantra, over and over, until he should have gotten it right.

Even as his old red pickup sped toward town late Tuesday morning, he was muttering it to himself, swearing that he'd have lunch with Luke and Jordan at Rosa's Mexican Café, then turn right around and go back to White Pines. A couple of beers and a plate of Rosa's spiciest food would wipe all thoughts of Melissa straight out of his head.

Unfortunately he hadn't counted on his brothers getting into the act. He'd been certain that they would leave the subject of his love life alone. He hadn't counted on the fact that both of them were now happily married and apparently intent on seeing that he took the plunge, too.

"Hey, Cody, why don't you drop by Dolan's as long as you're in town?" Jordan suggested after they'd eaten. He said it with all the innocence of Harlan at his matchmaking best.

"Any particular reason I should?" he inquired, re-fusing to fall into Jordan's trap.

He lifted the cold bottle of beer to his lips and took a long, slow drink just to show how unaffected he was by the prospect of seeing Melissa, whom Jordan clearly knew worked at Dolan's. This was probably the whole reason his brothers had suggested meeting in town in the first place rather than gathering at White Pines. They'd been plotting behind his back to try to force a reunion between Cody and his ex-lover.

"They still have the best milk shakes in the whole state of Texas," Luke chimed.

"We've just eaten enough food to stuff a horse," Cody stated flatly.

Luke and Jordan exchanged a look.

"Worried about your handsome figure?" Luke taunted.

Cody scowled at his oldest brother's nonsense. "No."

Luke went on as if he'd never spoken. "Because if that's it, I'm sure they have diet sodas in there, served up by the sweetest gal in all of Texas, or so I hear."

"I don't want a milk shake. I don't want a diet soda. There is nothing that drugstore has that I want," he said pointedly, scowling first at Luke and then at Jor-dan.

"Sounds to me like a man who's protesting too much," Jordan observed. "What does it sound like to you, Lucas?"

"Definitely a man who's scared out of his britches," Luke agreed.

Cody drew himself up indignantly. "Scared of what? A milk shake?"

"Maybe not that," Luke conceded. "How about Melissa Horton?"

Ah, a direct hit. Cody sighed. "I am not scared of Melissa," he said with extreme patience. "I feel absolutely nothing for Melissa."

"Cluck, cluck, cluck," Luke murmured, making a pitiful attempt to mimic a chicken.

The sound grated on Cody's nerves. He balled his hands into fists. He hadn't gotten into a rip-roaring fight with his big brothers in a very long time, but Luke was pushing every one of his buttons. And, from the teasing glint in his eyes, his big brother knew it, too. Even Jordan sensed that his patience was at an end. He eased his chair between them, a conciliatory expression on his face.

"Now, Luke, don't rile Cody," he said blandly. "If he says he doesn't want to talk to Melissa, then who are we to interfere?"

Cody didn't exactly trust Jordan's sudden taking of his side. Jordan had a knack for sneak attacks that could cripple a business adversary before he even knew he was under seige. Cody eyed him warily.

"That's true," Luke conceded, his turnaround just as suspicious. "Daddy meddled in our lives enough that we should be more sensitive to Cody's feelings. Besides, Melissa probably doesn't want to see him any more than he wants to see her."

"Why? Is she involved with someone?" Cody asked, regretting the words the instant they slipped out of his mouth. The triumphant expressions on Luke's and Jordan's faces were enough to set his teeth on edge.

Jordan stood as if he'd just recalled a business crisis that couldn't be put off. "Come on, Luke. We've obviously accomplished our mission here," he said blithely. "The man is on the hook. Let's leave him to decide whether to wiggle off or take the bait."

"A fascinating metaphor," Luke commented, joining Jordan. He glanced back at Cody. The teasing glint in his eyes faded. "Don't be a damned fool, little brother. Go see the woman. You know you want to. It's time you settled things with her once and for all. We want you back here for good."

Cody finished the beer after they'd gone. He thought about ordering another one, but decided against it. It would only be delaying the inevitable. Some sick, perverse part of him wanted to see Melissa, just as Luke had guessed. He needed to know if that reaction he'd felt at the church had been a fluke or the undeniable response of a man for the woman he'd belatedly realized that he'd always loved.

He paid the check—his damned brothers had stiffed him on the bill, on top of everything else—and then headed down Main Street. In the middle of the block he hesitated, staring across at the front of the drugstore that had been his favorite hangout as a teenager. His and Melissa's.

Little had changed. Dolan's Drugstore was still printed in neat black, gold-edged letters on the door. A display of toys sat on the shelf beneath the big plate-glass window, visible to any child passing by. A rack of comic books stood off to the side. Cody suspected they were the same faded editions that had been there a decade before. The toys looked suspiciously familiar, too. In fact, when he'd crossed the street for a closer look, he was almost certain that there was a ten-year layer of dust on the red, toy fire truck.

Telling himself he was fifty kinds of crazy for going inside, he found himself turning the knob on the door anyway. A bell tinkled overhead, alerting anyone working that a customer had entered.

The soda fountain was on his left, partially blocked by a section of shelves with first-aid supplies and a new display of condoms. Talk about times changing. He couldn't think of a better example. He recalled the first time he'd ever come into the store to buy condoms. They'd been behind the pharmacy counter then. He'd blushed brick red when he'd had to ask Mabel Hastings to give them to him. It was a wonder he'd ever gone back. His only consolation had been that she'd seemed even more embarrassed. After that he'd always made sure Eli was on duty when he'd returned for a new supply.

A half-dozen teenage girls were sitting on one side of the U-shaped soda fountain, probably discussing schoolwork, or, more likely, boys. An equal number of boys was on the opposite side, tongue-tied and uncertain. The sight of them brought back a slew of memories best forgotten.

There was no sign of Melissa, though clearly someone had served the kids their shakes and hamburgers. Cody fought a bitter feeling of disappointment. He hadn't wanted to come here, but now that he had gathered the courage, he wanted to get this encounter out of the way. He wanted to shove the past behind him once and for all. He doubted a meeting would be enough to keep him in Texas, but maybe it would buy him some peace of mind.

"Hey, Missy, customer!" one of the boys shouted as Cody slid onto a stool close to the cash register.

"I'll be right there," a voice capable of raising goose bumps on any man past puberty sang out from the back.

The door to the storeroom swung open. Melissa emerged, her arms loaded with two trays of glasses piled atop each other. Her gaze zeroed in on Cody with impeccable precision. Every bit of color washed from her face. The trays wobbled, then tilted. Glasses crashed to the floor. Her gaze never wavered from his, despite the sound of breaking glass.

Several of the teenagers sprang to their feet and rushed to clean up the mess. Cody couldn't have moved if his life had depended on it. Apparently Melissa couldn't, either. Not even the swirl of activity at her feet caught her attention. He felt as if he'd been punched in the gut.

This definitely wasn't the reaction he'd been praying for. In fact, it was exactly the opposite. He'd wanted to look into those soft, sea green eyes of hers and feel eighteen months of hurt and anger boiling into a fine rage. Or, better yet, he'd wanted to feel nothing at all.

Instead it appeared his hormones were very glad to see her. Obviously they had a different sort of memory pattern than his brain.

"Missy, are you okay?" one of the boys asked worriedly. He scowled in Cody's direction.

"Fine," she murmured.

The youngster, who looked all of fourteen, clearly wasn't convinced. Just as clearly, he had a big-time crush on Melissa. "Is he a problem?" he inquired, nodding toward Cody.

Apparently the boy's itch to slay dragons for her got her attention as nothing else had. She jerked her gaze away from Cody and smiled at the teenager.

"It's okay, David. Cody and I have known each other a long time." She patted his shoulder. "Thanks for cleaning up the glass, you guys. Your sodas are on me."

"Nah, you don't have to do that," David said, pulling money out of his pocket and leaving it on the counter. "Right, guys?"

The other boys dutifully nodded and pulled out their own cash. Unless costs at Dolan's had risen dramatically, they were very generous tippers, Cody noted as all of the teens departed.

"See you tomorrow," David called back from the doorway. He lingered uncertainly for another minute, as if he couldn't make up his mind whether Cody was to be trusted. When Melissa shot him another reassuring smile, he finally took off to catch up with his friends.

"Quite an admirer," Cody said. "I think he was ready to mop up the floor with me."

"David is just testing his flirting skills. I'm safer than those girls in his own class. He knows I won't laugh at him."

"Maybe you should. Better to hurt him now than later," he said with unmistakable bitterness.

Melissa looked as if he'd struck her. "I'm not going to hurt him at all. He's just a boy, Cody." She straightened her spine and glowered at him. "Look, if you came in here just to hassle me, you can turn right around and go back wherever you came from. I don't need the aggravation."

Cody grinned at the bright patches of color in her cheeks. Melissa had always had a quick temper. He suddenly realized he'd missed sparring with her almost as much as he'd missing making love with her.

"Actually, I came in for a milk shake," he said, coming to a sudden decision to play this scene all the way through. He propped his elbows on the counter. He waited until he'd caught her gaze, then lowered his voice to a seductive whisper. "A chocolate shakc so thick, I'll barely be able to suck it very, very slowly through the straw."

The patches of color in Melissa's cheeks deepened. She twirled around so fast it was a wonder she didn't knock a few more pieces of glassware onto the floor with the breeze she stirred.

With her rigid back to him, Cody was able to observe her at his leisure. Her snug, faded jeans fit her cute little butt like a glove. That much hadn't changed, he noted with satisfaction. With every stretch, the cropped T-shirt she wore kept riding up to bare an intriguing inch or so of a midriff so perfect that it could make a man weep. Her long dark hair with its shimmering red highlights had been scooped up in a saucy ponytail that made her look a dozen years younger than the twenty-seven he knew she was.

And, to his very sincere regret, she made him every bit as hard now as she had as a teenager. He squirmed in a wasted effort to get more comfortable on the vinyl-covered stool.

When she finally turned back, she plunked his milk shake onto the counter with such force half of it sloshed out of the tall glass. Apparently she wasn't entirely immune to him, either, and she wasn't one bit happier about the discovery.

She grabbed up a dishrag and began scrubbing the opposite side of the counter, her back to him. Given the energy she devoted to the task, the surface was either very dirty or she was avoiding him.

"So, how've you been?" Cody inquired, managing the nonchalant tone with supreme effort.

"Fine," she said tersely, not even glancing around.

He frowned. Why the hell was she acting like the injured party here? She was the one who'd cheated on him. Getting her to meet him halfway became an irresistible challenge.

"How are you, Cody? It's been a long time," he coached.

She turned and glared. "Why are you here?" she demanded instead.

He could have shot back a glib retort, but he didn't. He actually gave the question some thought. He considered the teasing he'd gotten from Jordan and Luke. He considered his own undeniable curiosity. He even considered the size of his ego, which had found being cheated on damned hard to take. The bottom line was, he had no idea what had drawn him across the street and into the drugstore.

"I don't know," he finally admitted.

Apparently it was the right answer because her lush, kissable mouth curved into a smile for the first time since she'd spotted him at the counter.

"You mean to tell me that there's something that actually stymies the brilliant, confident Cody Adams?"

He nodded slowly. "It surprises the dickens out of me, too."

She leaned back against the counter, her elbows propped behind her. It was a stance that drew attention to her figure, though Cody doubted she was aware of it.

"You planning on sticking around?" she asked.

"A few more days, just till Daddy's got his feet back under him again." It was the same response he'd given everyone who'd asked. Now that he was right here with Melissa in front of him, though, he wondered if she might not be the one person who could change his mind.

At the mention of his father, her expression immediately filled with concern. "It must be horrible for him."

"It is."

"And the rest of you?"

"We're doing okay. Mostly we're worried about Daddy. He adored Mother. It's going to be lonely as hell for him with her gone."

"I'm surprised you're not staying, then."

He shook his head. "There's nothing for me here anymore," he said automatically, refusing to concede that he had evidence to the contrary in the tightening of his groin at the first sight of her.

She actually blanched at his harsh words. "I'm sorry," she whispered, looking shaken. "What about White Pines? You always loved it. You were building your whole future around running that ranch."

She was right about that. He'd fought tooth and nail to get Harlan to trust him with the running of the ranch. He'd spent his spare time building his own house on the property just to make the point that, unlike Luke or Jordan, he never intended to leave. Then in a matter of seconds after catching Melissa with Brian, he'd thrown it all away.

Now, rather than addressing his longing to be working that land again, he shoved those feelings aside and clung instead to the bitterness that had sent him away.

"There's no way I can stay here now," he said, unable to prevent the accusing note that had crept into his voice. "You ruined it for me."

Melissa swallowed hard, but she kept her gaze on him steady. Some part of him admired her for not backing down.

"Maybe we should talk about what happened, Cody. Maybe if we could put it behind us, you'd change your mind about staying. Your decision to stay or go shouldn't have anything to do with me."

Talk about finding her in the arms of his best friend? Analyze it and pick it apart, until his emotions were raw? Cody practically choked on the idea. Once he got started on that subject, he doubted the conversation would remain polite or quiet. Eli would be bolting out from behind the prescription counter and Mabel, whom he'd spotted lurking over toward the cosmetics, would get a blistering earful.

No, he absolutely did not want to talk about the past. Or the present. And most definitely not about the bleak, lonely future he'd carved out for himself.

He slid off the stool and backed up a step. "There's nothing to say," he said, hoping his tone and his demeanor were forbidding enough to keep Melissa silent. He slapped a five on the counter, then tipped his hat.

"It's been a pleasure," he said in a tone that declared just the opposite.

He had made it almost to the door when he heard a soft gasp of dismay behind him. He stepped aside just as Velma Horton opened the door and pushed a stroller inside. His gaze went from Velma's shocked expression to the chubby-cheeked little girl who promptly reached her arms up toward him, a thoroughly engaging smile on her face. He stared at the toddler in stunned silence, then pivoted slowly to stare at Melissa. Her face was ashen, removing any doubt at all that the baby was hers.

For the second time in a matter of minutes Cody felt as if he'd been hit below the belt. He could count backward as quickly as anyone in Texas. That darling little girl with the big eyes and innocent smile looked to be a year old, which meant she was Brian's.

His blood felt like ice water in his veins, but he forced himself to walk back toward the soda fountain. "I see congratulations are in order," he said so politely it made his teeth ache. "Your daughter is beautiful."

"Thank you," Melissa said so softly that he could barely hear her.

"I guess you and Brian were meant to be, after all," he said, then turned on his heel and bolted for the door before he made an absolute idiot of himself.

He brushed past Velma and the baby without giving them a second glance. Damn, Melissa! She'd turned him inside out again. For a fleeting moment he'd actually wondered if he could put the past behind him and move on, maybe get something going with her again since his body was as hot for her now as it had been eighteen months ago. He'd allowed old feelings to stir to life, indulged in a few quick and steamy fantasies.

One look at that baby had shattered any possibility of that. He should have known that Melissa and Brian were together. He should have guessed that the betrayal was more serious than the one-night stand he'd tried desperately to convince himself it was. He should have realized that neither of them would have cheated on him for anything less than powerful emotions they couldn't control. He should have given them credit for that much at least. He couldn't make up his mind, though, if that should make him feel better or worse.

It wasn't until he was back at White Pines, riding hell-bent for leather across the open land trying to work off his anger and his pain that he stopped to wonder why Jordan and Luke would have set him up for such a terrible sucker punch. Couldn't they just have told him and saved him the anguish of making a fool of himself over Melissa all over again?

Instead they had taunted him into going into Dolan's. They had poked and prodded at all of his old feelings for Melissa until he could no longer ignore them. Would they have done that if they'd known about Brian? If they'd known about the baby? Harlan had done his share of nudging, too. He'd been the first to plant the seed about finding Melissa at Dolan's.

It didn't make a lick of sense. How could they not have known? It was a small town. Harlan sure as hell knew everything that went on. And yet they had sent him like a lamb to slaughter, straight back to Melissa.

He reined in his horse and sat for a long time contemplating the possibilities. For once in his life he was oblivious to the raw beauty of the land surrounding him. Since he knew damned well his brothers weren't cruel, their actions had to mean something. At the very least, he'd bet that Melissa and Brian weren't married, after all. At the most . . .

He thought of that cute little girl who'd practically begged him to pick her up.

He didn't even want to consider the astonishing, incredible idea that had just popped into his head. What if she was his? What if he was actually a father?

He tried the idea on for size and realized that a silly grin had spread across his face. A father? Yes, indeed, the possibility fit as well as those tight little jeans had caressed Melissa's fanny.

Then his grin faded as he considered all the time he'd lost if it were true. If that little girl was his, he resolved there was going to be hell to pay.

Chapter Four

Melissa stood over Sharon Lynn's crib and stared down at her sleeping child. The baby's cheeks were flushed, her dark blond hair curling damply against her chubby neck. Her blue nightshirt was sprinkled with tiny yellow ducks. A larger, stuffed duck was cuddled next to her. It had been her favorite toy ever since she'd been to a duck pond a few months before. She refused to go to bed without it.

A smile curved Melissa's lips as she watched her baby and fought the desperate need to pick her up, to cling to her. She hadn't been able to let her daughter out of her sight since that terrible moment in the drugstore when Cody had come face-to-face with his child. In that instant her heart had ricocheted wildly and her breath had caught in her throat as she'd waited for him to recognize Sharon Lynn as his, just as Jordan had the very first time he'd spotted her. She'd almost been grateful that the decision to tell Cody or not to tell him had been taken out of her hands.

But instead of promptly recognizing the baby as his, Cody had clearly leapt to the conclusion that someone else was the father. Given the cold glint in his eyes when he'd stepped back to the counter to congratulate her in a voice devoid of emotion and his comment about her relationship with Brian having been meant to be, he must have assumed the father was Brian Kincaid. It was a further complication in an already complicated situation.

She sighed as she considered the terrible mess she had made of things. She should have told Cody everything straight off, right then and there, but her mother's terrified expression and her earlier dire warnings had kept Melissa silent, too fearful of the consequences of blurting out the truth.

She couldn't imagine what her life would be like without her baby. As difficult as things had gotten after she'd learned she was pregnant, there had never been a single instant when she'd regretted having Cody's child. Every time she looked into that precious face, she saw a miracle that she and Cody had created together. Beyond that biological tie, however, Cody had no right at all to claim his child. She was the only parent Sharon Lynn had ever known. If only she could keep it that way.

Unfortunately, though, there was no way the truth could be kept hidden forever. Cody had already seen his daughter. His brother knew that Sharon Lynn was Cody's. Sooner or later the pieces of the puzzle would come together, and when they did, she didn't have a doubt in her mind what Cody's reaction would be. If he'd been furious when he'd thought she was cheating on him with his best friend, he would destroy her when he found out about the baby she'd kept from him. Maybe he wouldn't fight her for custody as her mother feared, but he would make her life into the hell she deserved for deceiving him in the first place.

She rubbed her knuckles against Sharon Lynn's soft skin and sighed again. There was so much of Cody in her daughter. She had the same stubborn tilt to her chin, the same dark blond hair that streaked with gold in the summer sun. And, for the most part, she had the same sunny disposition and laughing eyes Cody had had before he thought Melissa had betrayed him.

It had hurt today to glimpse the old teasing Cody, only to see him vanish in the space of a heartbeat at the first mention of the past. When he'd walked out of Dolan's, her heart had been heavy with the burden of guilt and fear.

"I have to be the one to tell him," she whispered finally, her fingers caressing that precious cheek. "I have to tell your daddy all about you."

Maybe by revealing the truth herself, before he learned it from someone else, she would have some small chance of earning his forgiveness. They could work out a solution together.

Tomorrow, she vowed. First thing tomorrow afternoon when she got off work, she would drive out to

White Pines and tell Cody everything. And then she would pray that it didn't cost her the only person on earth she held dear.

Too restless to stay in one place for long as he contemplated how to go about discovering whether Melissa's baby was his, Cody drove over to visit Jordan and Kelly. Six-year-old Dani was always a distraction and he just might get a chance to hold that nephew of his. He had a hunch it would be a bittersweet sensation given what he suspected about Melissa's child being his own.

"Uncle Cody!" Dani screamed when she caught sight of him. She ran and leapt into his arms, planting kisses all over his face. "I really, really missed you."

The weight of her in his arms, the peppermint-sticky kisses, filled him with nostalgia and accomplished exactly what he'd hoped for. "I really missed you, too, pumpkin. I'm sorry I didn't get to take those kittens you had for me awhile back."

She patted his cheek consolingly. "That's okay. Francie had more. Want to see? One is all black with a white nose. I think you'll really, really like him."

He grinned. "I bet I will," he agreed. "We'll go see him later."

"We'd better go now," Dani protested. "Later it will be my bedtime."

"Give me a few minutes inside to say hello to your mom," he negotiated. "I'm sure it won't be your bedtime then."

Dani braced her hands against his chest, leaned back in his arms and studied him intently. "You promise you won't leave without going to see the kittens?"

"I promise," he said, solemnly crossing his heart as he put her down.

"Okay," she said cheerfully, and ran toward the house screaming, "Mommy, Uncle Cody's here and he says he's going to take one of Francie's kittens."

"Thank goodness," Kelly called back as she emerged from the house, a grin on her face. "Conned you again, huh?"

He chuckled. "If you're not careful, that child of yours is going to be the biggest scam artist in the entire United States."

"I prefer to think she'll have a career in diplomacy or maybe negotiating strike settlements," Kelly said. "Come on in. Jordan's still at the office, but he should be home soon."

His sister-in-law surveyed him closely. "How are you? You look lousy."

"Obviously Dani isn't the only one in the family with a silver tongue."

Kelly didn't bat an eye. "Did you see Melissa today?"

"I'm sure you know perfectly well that your husband and Luke badgered me into it."

"They said they were going to try. I wasn't sure if it had worked."

"I saw her," he admitted. "And her baby." He watched closely for Kelly's reaction. She remained expressionless.

"I see," she said blandly, keeping her attention focused on the vegetables she was chopping. "How did it go?"

Cody thought she was working awfully darned hard to feign disinterest. "Fine for the first few minutes, ugly after that."

"Oh, Cody," she protested softly. "Isn't it time you settled things with her and came home for good?"

Suddenly he didn't want to pursue the topic. He needed a break from it. They could get into it again when Jordan got home. Hopefully his brother would have answers that Kelly couldn't or wouldn't give him.

"I don't want to talk about Melissa right now. First I want to catch a glimpse of that brand new baby boy of yours," he declared just as Jordan came in and dropped a kiss on his wife's cheek.

"Hey, little brother, what brings you by?" Jordan asked, sneaking a carrot from the pile Kelly had just cut up.

"He's going to take a kitten," Dani chimed in. "Can we go see them now, Cody? It's later."

Since going to see the kittens would keep him from having to deal with the subject of Melissa and her baby a little longer, Cody stood and headed for the kitchen door. Dani tucked her hand in his.

"You should probably take two kittens," she said on the way out. "One might get lonely."

"Listen, young lady, I said one kitten," he protested over the sound of Kelly and Jordan's laughter.

"But you were going to take two last time." Apparently she caught his stern expression because she gave a little shrug of resignation. "I bet you'll change your mind when you see them."

A half hour later he was back in the kitchen with two kittens in a box. Dani had been giving him very precise instructions on caring for them ever since they'd left the barn. Kelly's expression turned smug when she saw him.

"You are pitiful," Jordan said, shaking his head. "Is there a female on the face of the earth you can resist?"

"Who are you kidding?" Cody shot back, gesturing to the big tomcat that was curled in Jordan's lap purring contentedly. "You always hated cats and now you're surrounded by them. I don't hear you complaining."

"You may not hear it," Kelly said, "but it is almost the last thing I hear every single night. He says 'Good night, I love you, no more cats,' all in one breath."

"I do not," Jordan said, dislodging the cat and pulling Kelly onto his lap.

Cody listened to their banter and watched their undisguised affection with envy. Until he'd lost Melissa he'd never thought he wanted marriage and kids. He'd been as commitment-phobic as any one of those jerks who made the rounds of the talk shows. Ironically, ever since their breakup, all he'd been able to think about was settling down and having kids. He'd deliberately isolated himself in Wyoming so he'd be far from the temptation to try something at which he knew he'd inevitably fail.

After all, he hadn't appreciated Melissa when he'd had her and she was as sexy and generous, as kind and intelligent, as any woman he'd ever known. He'd had a roving eye, just the same. He'd taken her for granted, which everyone in the family had accused him of doing at one time or another. He suspected he'd do the same with a wife. What was the point of ruining some woman's life for his own selfish longing to have just a taste of the kind of love Jordan and Luke had found?

"How long are you sticking around? Have you told your boss when you'll be back in Wyoming?" Jordan asked after Kelly insisted Cody stay for dinner.

Kelly dished up a serving of stew for him and lingered at his shoulder. "You are not going back until after J.J. is baptized," she said emphatically.

Cody glanced up at her. "When is that again?"

"Next weekend, which you know perfectly well. I sent you an invitation. We're going ahead with it. Harlan insisted."

Something in his expression must have given him away because she frowned. "You ripped it up, didn't you?"

Cody recalled the scattered pieces of the pretty blue invitation and felt a tide of red rising in his cheeks. Was the woman a damned witch?

"Of course not," he fibbed.

The response drew a disbelieving snort. "So you'll be here at least that long," she said.

Cody had a feeling once he learned the truth about Melissa's baby, he wouldn't be able to get away from Texas fast enough. He'd need to cool his temper for a good long while before confronting her with what he knew. He'd also need time to make up his mind exactly what he wanted to do about the baby she'd kept from him. He intended to learn that truth in the next twenty-four hours.

"Sorry," he said eventually. "I can't promise to stay that long."

Kelly glanced at Jordan, then back at him. "Your brothers said you were going to say no," she said.

"I had no idea I was so predictable."

"Lately you are," his sister-in-law said. "Lately, you've gotten downright boring."

He gave her a wry look. "More of that fatal charm, I see."

Kelly frowned at his teasing. "What if I told you that Jordan and I want you to be the baby's godfather?"

Something deep inside him shifted at the offer. He felt an unexpected warm glow. It was a feeling he told himself he didn't deserve, especially not if he had a real child of his own he'd never even acknowledged.

"I'd say you made a lousy choice," he responded.

"I told you he wouldn't even be gracious about it," Jordan chimed in. "Leave him be, Kelly. He's as stubborn as the rest of us when he digs in his heels. He'll change his mind, if we let the idea simmer long enough."

"I won't change my mind," Cody said. "Sorry."

"You say that a lot these days," Jordan observed.

"Maybe I have a lot to be sorry for."

"Well, this is one thing you can check off the list," Jordan said.

He spoke in that matter-of-fact way that indicated he'd reached a decision and wanted no further argument. It was a tactic that might have served him well in business, but it grated on Cody's nerves.

"I want you here, little brother," Jordan stated emphatically. "And I want you to be the baby's godfather. It's settled."

Despite his annoyance at Jordan's attempt to snatch the decision out of his hands, Cody could feel himself weakening, feel that odd, empty sensation in the pit of his stomach that always meant the loneliness was taking hold again.

"Did you check it out at the church?" he inquired lightly. "They'll probably be worried about lightning hitting the steeple if I show my hide in there."

"There was some mention of that, but I believe there's a general consensus that your soul is still salvageable," Kelly said. "Please, Cody. We've missed you. It's only for a few days more. How bad can that be?"

A few days, one hour, any time at all would be hell, especially if he discovered in the meantime that he had a baby of his own. Still, Cody had never been able to resist his sister-in-law. Kelly had been coaxing him into trouble since they were toddlers. Jordan had been too stuffy even at seven to fall in with some of her more outrageous mischief, though there had never been a doubt in anyone's mind that Jordan was the one she loved.

"I'll stick around," he said eventually. "Long enough to get that nephew of mine in good graces with the Lord. Then I'm heading right back out. Understood?''

"Understood," Kelly said meekly.

Kelly meek? Every alarm bell in him went off. Before he could get too caught up in trying to figure out her angle, she was gone. He was left alone with Jordan, while Kelly went upstairs to tuck Dani into bed. Suddenly the questions that had been tormenting him earlier in the day could no longer be ignored.

"Kelly mentioned that you saw Melissa and her little girl today, after you left Luke and me," Jordan said, his gaze fixed on Cody's face.

The comment gave him the perfect opening. "Why didn't you warn me?" Cody asked, trying to keep the anger out of his voice. "You knew about the baby, didn't you?"

Jordan sighed, then nodded. "I saw her once, about eight months ago. She was just a baby." He scanned Cody's face as if looking for answers. "What did you think when you saw her?"

"I figured Melissa and Brian had more going for them than I'd realized. I figured they were a happy little family now." Cody threw out the possibility to gauge his brother's reaction. If Jordan knew anything different, he'd find it out now.

The color washed out of Jordan's face. "Did you say that to Melissa?"

"More or less," he admitted. "Along with offering her my congratulations."

"What did she say?"

"Nothing."

"I see."

Cody lost patience for the game. He knew darned well that Jordan knew more than he was saying. He could see it in his eyes. His brother was looking everywhere in the kitchen except directly at him.

"You might as well spit it out," he told him finally.

"What?"

"Whatever has you looking like you'd rather be in Kansas."

A faint grin tugged at Jordan's mouth. "Maybe Houston, not Kansas," he said. He sighed. "How good a look did you get at the child?"

"Good enough," Cody said. He sensed that Jordan wanted him to reach a different conclusion than he'd just offered all on his own. He sucked in a deep breath. "She's mine, isn't she?"

Once Cody had actually spoken the words out loud, Jordan nodded, confirming everything.

Cody's heart pounded. An uncommon mix of hope and dismay swirled through him. "You know that for sure?"

"I saw it right off," Jordan admitted. "She was the spitting image of your baby pictures. I confronted Melissa about it straight out."

Cody felt an icy chill settle over him as Jordan's earlier comment came back to him. He stood and leaned down to look his brother in the eye. "And that was when? About eight months ago, you said?"

"Yes," Jordan replied softly.

"And Melissa confirmed your suspicions right then and there?" he demanded, the hurt and anger of yet another betrayal slamming through him.

"Yes."

"Damn you, Jordan," he snapped, backing up to prevent slamming a fist in his brother's face. "How could you do that to me? How could you keep a secret like that? Didn't you think I had a right to know? Or was this another one of those big-brother-knows-best decisions?"

"She pleaded with me not to tell you," Jordan said simply.

Cody stared at him incredulously. "And your loyalty was with her and not me?"

"Why the hell do you think I've done everything in my power to get you back here? I didn't want to lay this on you when you were in Wyoming. I wanted you here, so you could see for yourself. I didn't want you to accuse me or her of making it up just to get you back here."

Cody wasn't buying it. "No, you were more concerned with keeping your promise to a woman who betrayed me than you were with doing what was right—giving me a chance to know my own child." He turned on his heel and headed for the door, the box of kittens in tow. "I can't believe you would do something like this. Maybe family loyalty doesn't mean anything once you're a big corporate executive. Is that it, big brother?"

"Cody, you have it all wrong," Kelly protested when she came back into the kitchen. Obviously she had overheard the tail end of the argument.

"I don't think so," he snapped, shooting her a look of regret. "Don't expect me at the baptism, after all. In fact, forget you even know me."

Kelly called out after him. He heard the screen door slam behind her, then Jordan murmuring something he couldn't quite make out. Whatever it was, though, it silenced her. When he looked back as he drove away, he saw them standing on the porch staring after him. He was sure it was only his imagination, but he thought he saw his brother wiping something that might have been tears from his cheeks.

He slowed the car momentarily and closed his eyes against the tide of anguish washing through him. Melissa had done it again. She had come between him and his family. He vowed then and there it would be the last time. This time he wouldn't run. He wouldn't let her control his destiny as he had before.

Forgetting all about his resolve to let his temper cool, an hour later he was in town, pounding on the Hortons' front door. Ken Horton, wearing a robe and slippers, opened it a crack. At the sight of Cody, he swung it wider, a welcoming smile spreading across his weathered face. Cody could see Velma's panicky expression as she stared over her husband's shoulder.

"Cody, what on earth?" Horton grumbled. "You trying to wake the whole neighborhood?"

"Where's Melissa?"

"She's not here," he said as his wife tugged frantically on his arm. When he leaned down, she whispered something in his ear, something that wiped any lingering expression of welcome from his face. "Go on home, Cody."

"Not until you tell me where she is."

"Don't make me call the sheriff."

"Don't make me pound the information out of you," Cody shot back belligerently.

Ken Horton regarded him sympathetically. "Boy, go on home and get some sleep. If you've got things to talk over with Melissa, do it in the morning, when you're calmer."

Despite his earlier promise to himself to think things through clearly, Cody realized he didn't want to be calm when he talked to Melissa. He wanted this rage to keep him focused, to keep him immune to the sight of her. He wanted to have this out with her while he was hot with anger, not lust.

"If I have to knock on every door in town, I'm going to talk to her tonight," he swore.

"There's nothing you have to say, nothing you need to know, that won't be settled just as readily in the morning," Horton repeated, still calm, still intractable.

Cody considered it as much as an admission that he and Melissa had serious issues to resolve, such as his relationship to that baby. He gathered from the warning look Horton shot at his now tearful wife that they didn't entirely agree on whether Cody had the right to know the truth.

"Where can I find her in the morning?" he asked finally, resigned to the delay. They all knew he wouldn't tear through town, creating yet another ruckus he'd never live down.

"She gets to work about nine," her father told him.

"I'm not talking to her at Dolan's," he said. "I don't want the whole town knowing our business."

Horton seemed about to offer an alternative when Velma piped up. "That'll just have to do," she said. "We're not telling you where she lives."

He couldn't decide if Velma was worried about him throttling Melissa or if she was simply being protective of her daughter's secret. Because he wasn't sure, he backed down.

"If you talk to her, let her know I'll be by the minute the doors open. Tell her to arrange with Eli for someone to cover for her unless she wants her personal life broadcast to everyone in town."

To his surprise, Ken Horton held out his hand. When Cody shook it, Melissa's father said, "For whatever it's worth, Cody, I think it's about time you two got everything out in the open. The two of you had something special once. Melissa's been punished enough for making one foolish mistake."

He gave his wife a defiant look. "And a man has a right to claim his child."

Velma Horton groaned and covered her face with her hands. Tears spilled down her cheeks. Cody wondered at the fear he'd seen in her eyes right before she placed her hands over them. She'd had the same terrified expression earlier in the day. He'd always thought Velma

Horton liked him. Now she seemed to think he was some sort of a monster.

Was she blaming him for running out on her pregnant daughter? Or was it something more? He wondered what could possibly be behind the expression he'd read in her eyes.

Eventually, as he slowly walked back to his pickup, it came to him. She was actually afraid that he'd come home to take his baby away from Melissa.

Was that what he intended? He sat in his truck on the dark street in front of the Hortons' house, his head resting on the steering wheel. He honestly hadn't thought beyond discovering the truth and confronting Melissa with it.

Obviously, it was a good thing Ken Horton had prevented him from seeing Melissa tonight. He needed to get his thoughts in order. He needed to have a plan. For once in his life he couldn't act on impulse. Too many lives were at stake, his own, Melissa's, and that darling little girl's.

His heart ached every time he thought about his daughter. His arms felt empty, just as they did when Dani climbed out of them or he had to turn Angela back over to Jessie or Luke. He wondered about that vacant place he'd thought would always be inside him and realized that there was someone who could fill it, a child of his own.

Tomorrow he would claim her. He realized he didn't even know her name or how old she was or whether she could walk or talk. So many precious details. He sighed. Tomorrow he would fill in the gaps.

Tomorrow he would finally experience what it was like to feel like a father. Right now it was all too abstract, but in the morning he would hold his child in his arms. Whatever else happened between him and Melissa, he vowed that nothing would ever rip his baby away from him again.

Chapter Five

Her mother had warned her. In fact, the first thing out of Velma's mouth when Melissa had dropped off her daughter for the day had been a detailed description of Cody's late-night visit. Based on Velma's panicked reaction, Melissa had been tempted to take Sharon Lynn and flee. She knew, though, that in his present mood Cody would only track her down.

Besides, hadn't she resolved just last night to tell him herself about Sharon Lynn? The decision on the timing had just been taken out of her hands. Of course, that also meant that his anger had had all night to simmer. She walked to work, dreading the confrontation that was clearly only minutes away.

She meant to ask Eli for an hour or so off to deal with a personal matter. She meant to be outside, on the sidewalk, when Cody arrived. She meant to do everything possible to ensure their conversation took place in private, away from prying eyes and potential gossip. She meant to be calm, reasonable, even conciliatory.

Cody took any chance of that out of her hands.

Before the door to the drugstore fully closed behind her, Melissa heard the bell ring loudly as the door slammed open again. Without even turning around, she sensed it was Cody. The air practically crackled with tension. She pivoted reluctantly and found him so close she could almost feel his breath on her face. She surveyed him slowly from head to toe, trying to gauge exactly how furious he was.

He looked exhausted. His mouth was set in a grim line. His shoulders were stiff. His hands were balled into fists. He also looked as if he'd slept in his clothes, perhaps in his truck, right in front of the drugstore. That would explain why he'd appeared right on her heels.

Despite all that, her heart flipped over. Her pulse scrambled. She had the most absurd desire to fling herself straight into his arms.

But she couldn't. More precisely, she didn't dare. It would only complicate an already impossible situation. She sucked in a deep breath and waited. The first move was going to have to be his.

As she waited, she was suddenly aware of every sound, every movement. She could hear the hum of the electric clock, the rattle of plastic bottles and *ping, ping, ping* of pills being counted out as Eli filled a prescription in the back, the swish of a mop as Mabel dusted the floor. Mabel rounded the aisle of shelves, caught sight of the silent tableau at the front of the store and stopped and stared.

Melissa felt like screaming. Mabel's presence was anticipated, but unfortunate. Of all the people in town, she was the most likely to spread word of every last detail of any encounter between Melissa and Cody. Her pale eyes sparkled as she watched the two of them.

Cody tipped his hat to Mabel, but didn't extend even that much courtesy to Melissa before latching on to her arm and practically hauling her into the storage room, past the startled gaze of Eli Dolan. Cody kicked the door shut behind them, plunging them into darkness.

"Dammit, Cody, what do you think you're doing?" Melissa demanded, trying to wrench herself free and reach the light switch at the same time. She couldn't succeed at doing either one.

"We need to talk," he declared, seemingly oblivious to the lack of light.

"Fine. Then let's do it like two civilized adults. There's no need for your caveman routine."

He was close enough that she could see that his eyes sparked fire, but he released his grip on her. Melissa felt along the wall until she found the switch. She flipped it on, illuminating the room that was small under the best of conditions, but claustrophobic with Cody pacing in the cramped space.

Somehow he managed to neatly avoid the stacks of just-delivered boxes, metal shelves of inventory and a disorderly array of cleaning supplies. Melissa had the feeling that he was practically daring the inanimate objects to give him an excuse to knock them all to the floor. She couldn't recall ever seeing him quite so angry or quite so speechless. Cody's glib tongue was known far and wide, especially among women.

She kept silent and waited. Finally he stopped in front of her, his hands shoved in his pockets, legs spread, a belligerent expression on his handsome face.

"Whose baby is it?" he demanded in a tone that made her hackles rise.

Melissa made up her mind then and there that she wasn't giving in to his bullying or to any coaxing he might decide to try when that failed. Maybe that had been the problem in the past. She'd been too darned easy on him, too much in love to ever say no. She hoisted her chin a challenging notch. They were going to have a conversation on her terms for a change.

"Good morning to you, too, Cody."

Cody's gaze narrowed at the sarcasm. "Dammit, I asked you a straight question. The least you could do is give me a straight answer."

She wasn't sure where she found the courage to face him down, but she did. "Why should I, when you're acting like a bully?"

"I think I have a right to act any damn way I please."

"No," she said softly. "You don't. I told you before that we can discuss this like two civilized adults or I can go into the other room and go to work."

He raked his hand through his hair in a gesture that was vintage Cody. She'd always been able to tell exactly how frustrated or annoyed he was by the disheveled state of his hair.

"If that baby's mine, I have a right to know," he retorted, his voice starting to climb.

"I was under the impression that you already know the answer to that. You certainly carried on as if you did when you dropped in on my parents last night."

He didn't look even vaguely chagrined by the reminder of his outrageous behavior on her parents' doorstep. "I want to hear it from you," he snapped. "I want to hear why you kept it from me. If I am that child's father, I should have been told about her way back when you first discovered you were pregnant. I had a right to know. We should have been making decisions together."

Melissa met his gaze unflinchingly. "You gave up any rights the day you left town without so much as a goodbye. You never got in touch. I didn't know where you were. How was I supposed to let you know?"

"Jordan knew where I was, but you made damned sure he wouldn't tell me, didn't you?"

"Because your leaving town the way you did told me everything I needed to know about how you felt about me. What was the point of dragging you back so you could tell me to kiss off?"

She could almost see his patience visibly snap.

"Dammit, Melissa, you know that I had more than enough cause to go," he practically shouted, slamming his fist into a box and sending it crashing to the floor. Judging from the shattering noise it made, it was the glasses Eli had bought to replace the supply she'd broken only the day before.

Eli opened the door a crack and peered inside, his expression anxious. "Everything okay back here?"

"Fine," Cody and Melissa said in unison. The response wasn't very heartfelt from either of them.

Eli glanced at the box on the floor and shook his head wearily. He backed away without comment and shut the door.

Throughout the interruption, Cody had kept his gaze fastened on her face, sending color flooding into her cheeks. "You know I'm right," he said more quietly the instant they were alone again. "You cheated on me."

She had known from the beginning that that was what he believed. She had even wanted him to believe it...up to a point. Even so, it hurt to hear him say it. "Still jumping to conclusions, I see. That was always one of your worst habits, Cody."

He shoved his fingers through his thick hair again. "Jumping to conclusions," he repeated incredulously. "Did you or did you not sleep with my best friend?"

She was amazed at the speed with which the conversation had veered from the subject of their daughter to the real source of Cody's fury. He'd had well over a year to work up a good head of steam on the subject and clearly he intended to vent it now, unless she put a quick stop to it.

"I did not," she told him quietly.

"See—" he began triumphantly. His expression suddenly faltered as her reply finally penetrated his thick skull. "You didn't?"

"Never," she said emphatically, her gaze unflinching.

"But I saw..."

"You saw exactly what I wanted you to see." She shrugged. "Unfortunately, you leapt to the wrong conclusion."

He stared at her blankly. "I don't get it."

It was time—way past time—to spell it out for him. "Brian and I had one date. It wasn't even a date, really. It was a setup. Brian only went along with it because he knew I was crazy about you. You were supposed to get wildly jealous, realize you were madly in love with me, and propose. You were supposed to fight for me. You weren't supposed to haul your butt out of town without looking back."

"Jealous?" He stared at her in bemusement. "How the hell was I supposed to know that? You were in his arms. What was I supposed to think, that you were discussing the weather?" he asked in a tone loud enough to wake the dead.

"You're shouting again," she observed.

He scowled. "Well, so what if I am?"

Melissa chuckled despite herself. He was too darned stubborn to recognize even what was staring him straight in the face, much less the subtleties of the trap she had tried to spring on him. No wonder it had failed so miserably. She should have issued an ultimatum in plain English if she'd wanted him to marry her, not tried to trick him into recognizing his own feelings. As for right now, he obviously needed his present circumstances clarified for him.

"Mabel's probably taking notes," she stated patiently. "Eli may be calling the sheriff. Other than that, there's no reason to quiet down that I can think of."

Cody groaned and sank onto a stack of boxes. When he finally looked at her again, she thought she detected a hint of wonder in his eyes.

"Then the baby really is mine?" he asked quietly. "Jordan was right?"

"No doubt about it, at least in anyone's mind except yours."

His gaze honed in on hers and an expression of complete awe spread over his face. "I have a baby."

"Actually, you have a *toddler,*" she corrected. "She's thirteen months old."

"Whatever," he said, clearly unconcerned with the distinction. "Tell me everything. I want to know her name. How long you were in labor. What time she was born. I want to know what she likes to eat, whether she can talk, how many steps she's taken, if she has allergies, what her favorite toy is. I want to know every last detail."

The yearning behind his words struck her. He almost sounded as if he regretted missing out on so much. His eagerness was impossible to resist. Suddenly she couldn't wait to see him with his daughter. It was something she'd dreamed about since the first moment the doctor had confirmed her pregnancy.

"Wouldn't you rather just go and meet her?" Melissa inquired softly.

He nodded, apparently speechless again.

"I'll speak to Eli and be right with you," she promised.

"Don't try ducking out the back," he warned, but he was grinning when he said it.

"I'm not the one who runs," she reminded him.

His comment might have been half-teasing, but hers was not. She wanted him to know that she was stronger now than she had been when he'd abandoned her. She wanted him to know that she was tough enough and secure enough to fight him for her daughter, if she had to.

But she also wanted him to see that she was brave enough to allow him into his child's life, if he wanted a place there. This wasn't about her any longer. It wasn't about her feelings for Cody, though those clearly hadn't died. This was about her daughter and what was best for her. It was about giving her child a chance to know her father.

Even so, as they walked down Main Street toward the tree-lined street where her family had lived her whole life, Melissa couldn't help the vague stirring of hope deep inside her. The past year and a half of loneliness and regret had been wiped out of her heart in the blink of an eye. Left in its wake was anticipation, the eager-to-start-the-day anticipation of a woman in love. As dangerous an emotion as that was, she could no more have prevented it than she could have held back the wildness of a tornado's winds.

Cody was back and she might as well admit to herself one more truth. Time and distance hadn't dulled her feelings for him a bit. She wanted him every bit as fiercely as she ever had.

Cody was in a daze. He was only marginally aware of the woman walking beside him. Instead he kept seeing images of the child that he now knew without any doubt whatsoever was his. Melissa's confirmation kept echoing over and over in his head. He was a father.

The realization was both incredible and scary. What if he blew it? What if his daughter took one look at him and rejected him? Okay, the latter was unlikely. Just the day before she had reached for him as if she already knew who he was. He recalled the eager stretch of her arms in the air and the sensation of tenderness that had welled up inside him at her innocent smile.

On the walkway at the Hortons' he paused, his hand on Melissa's arm. "Wait."

She turned a quizzical look on him. "Second thoughts?"

"No." He swallowed hard. "What's her name?"

"Sharon Lynn."

He repeated it softly, just to hear how it sounded on his tongue. "I like it."

"I'm not sure she'll tolerate being called by both when she gets a little older, but for now that's what we call her. My father tends to call her Pookie. I'm trying to break him of the habit. I will not have my child go through life being nicknamed Pookie. Missy is bad enough.''

He smiled at her and barely resisted the urge to reach over and brush a strand of auburn hair from her cheek. ''I never called you Missy.''

''For which I was exceedingly grateful. That's probably why I let you get away with so much.''

''You never let me get away with a thing,'' he protested.

''That baby inside says otherwise.''

''I'll have to remember that,'' he said, grinning. ''If I just whisper your name in your ear, you'll do anything I ask, is that right?''

She frowned, probably at the sudden provocative note in his voice. He knew she didn't want him to guess how easily he got to her. She was going to fight him tooth and nail.

''That was then,'' she said staunchly, confirming his guess. ''This is now and the tide has turned, cowboy.''

He readily accepted the challenge in her tone. ''Is that so, Me…liss…a?'' He deliberately drew her name out. Before she could react to the teasing, he lowered his head and dropped a quick kiss on her parted lips. ''See, it still works.''

The startled, slightly dazed expression on her face almost tempted him to try again. That brief brush of his mouth over hers had been just enough to tantalize him. Memories of warm, moist kisses and stolen caresses slammed through him, turning teasing into something very, very serious.

How had he ever walked away from her? Why hadn't he stayed and fought, just as she'd demanded earlier? Had it been the gut-deep sense of betrayal that had driven him all the way to Wyoming? Or had it simply been the even more powerful fear of the commitment to which fighting for her would have led? He'd never thought of himself as a coward, but suddenly he was taking a long, hard look at his actions in a whole new light.

"Cody?"

He blinked and gazed down into her upturned face. Before he could question himself, he scooped his hand through her silky hair to circle the back of her neck. With his gaze fixed on her turbulent sea green eyes, he reclaimed her mouth, lingering this time, savoring, remembering.

He felt her hands on his chest, tentative at first, then more certain as she slid them up to his shoulders and clung. Her body fit itself neatly, automatically, into his, the movement as natural as breathing and far, far more exciting.

Cody couldn't believe he had ever walked away from this. He couldn't imagine how he had lived without the sweetness of her kisses or the heat of her body pressed against his. The swirl of sensations was overpowering, demanding...and totally inappropriate for a sidewalk in plain view, he realized as a passing car honked and the teenage driver shouted out encouragement.

Melissa backed away as if she'd been burned. Her face was flaming with embarrassment. A warning flashed in her eyes, turning them the shade of soft jade in sunlight.

"That can't happen again," she stated emphatically.

"It can and it will," Cody said with just as much certainty. "Count on it."

Alarm flared in her expression. "No, Cody, this isn't about you and me anymore."

"Sure it is, darlin'. It always was."

"No!" She practically shouted it, as if volume might make her edict clearer. "You and I are over. You saw to that."

Cody dropped his own voice to a seductive growl. "We'll see," he taunted.

"Dammit, Cody, do you or do you not want to see your daughter?"

"Of course I do," he said, amused that she seemed to think the two concepts were diametrically opposed. "Meeting Sharon Lynn has absolutely nothing to do with my intentions toward you."

"Yes, it does," she said stubbornly.

"You're not keeping me from my daughter," he responded emphatically. "And you're not going to put up much resistance, once I set my mind to winning you back."

A scowl darkened her face. "You are the most arrogant, most infuriating man on the face of the earth. It's too late, Cody. You couldn't win me back if you courted me from now till we're both tottering around in orthopedic shoes."

A grin tugged at his lips. "Is that a challenge?"

"That's a guarantee."

Chuckling at her sincere conviction that she could win a test of wills with him, he took her hand and headed for the house.

"You don't have a chance, sweet pea," he told her solemnly as he ushered her inside, where Velma was waiting, her gaze wary. He lowered his voice to taunt one last time, "You don't have a snowball's chance in hell."

Melissa never responded because her mother spoke up just then.

"You brought him," Velma said, her tone accusing.

"You knew I would," Melissa told her mother. "Where's Sharon Lynn?"

"Down for her nap," she said, a note of triumph in her voice. "There's no need to wake her."

Cody was aware of the undercurrents between mother and daughter. Clearly, Velma was angry about his presence. Once again he had the sense that she feared him having any contact at all with his child.

Melissa shot him a vaguely apologetic look. "I'll get her," she said.

He fell into step beside her. "Don't wake her. I'll come with you. Let me just look at her for now. Your mother's right. There's no need to wake her yet."

If he had expected the suggestion to gain Velma's approval, he failed. He should have saved his breath. An expression of doom on her face, she trailed along behind them. He had the feeling she would have thrown herself across the threshold to the bedroom if she'd thought it would keep him away from her grand-daughter.

He couldn't waste time worrying about Velma, though. From the instant he stepped into the room his gaze was riveted to the child asleep in the crib. She was sleeping on her stomach, her legs drawn up under her, her butt sticking up in the air. He couldn't imagine the position being comfortable, but she was sleeping soundly.

Awestruck, he moved closer to the crib. Melissa stayed a few steps behind him. Her mother never budged from the doorway. He studied the tiny, balled-up fists. Her skin looked soft as down and her light curls feathered around her face like wispy strands of silk. Her mouth curved like a miniature bow of pink. She was perfect. Adorable.

An overwhelming surge of protectiveness spread through him. This was his daughter. *His!* He'd seen Luke with the newborn Angela. He had watched Jordan hold J.J., but he had never guessed the depth of emotions that his brothers must have been feeling. He'd never experienced anything like it before in his life.

"She's so beautiful," he whispered, his voice choked.

"She has your eyes, your hair," Melissa said quietly.

"And your mouth," he noted. "I had no idea."

"No idea about what?"

"That it was possible to create anything so perfect."

Melissa laughed softly. "You haven't seen her throw a tantrum yet."

He turned toward her and grinned. "Ah, so she has your temper, too?"

"Oh, no," Melissa protested. "You're not blaming me for that. Every ounce of stubbornness she possesses she got from you."

Gazing directly into her eyes, he slipped an arm around her waist and pulled her close. "Thank you."

"For?"

He wasn't certain how to explain all that he was grateful to her for. For having the baby, even without him in her life. For keeping her healthy and safe. For loving her. So many things.

"For our daughter," he said simply.

"Oh, Cody," she whispered, tears welling up in her eyes and spilling down her cheeks.

"Shh, darlin', don't cry," he said, pulling her close. "You're not alone anymore."

To his astonishment, he realized that after the loneliest year and a half of his life, he was no longer alone, either. He was just a visit to the preacher away from having a family of his own. And nothing or no one was going to stand in his way.

Chapter Six

Still awestruck, Cody was knee-deep in mental wedding plans before he and Melissa walked out the front door of her parents' house. He was so caught up in thinking ahead to the day when Melissa and Sharon Lynn would move into his old house out at White Pines, that he almost forgot to ask Melissa to have dinner with him that night so he could officially propose and go over the details.

"Both of you," he told her as they stood in front of the drugstore a few minutes later. "You and Sharon Lynn. We'll go to DiPasquali's. I'll pick you up at your folks' place after you get off work."

Her lips set in a stubborn expression he knew only too well.

"Was there an invitation in there somewhere or did you mean it to sound like an order?" she asked.

He supposed they could quibble all morning over the difference, but he didn't see much point to it. They had far bigger issues to worry about, like setting a wedding date in the next week or so. Now that he'd seen his daughter, nothing was going to keep him from her. The prospect of instant parenthood scared the daylights out of him, but he was eager to get started, anxious to make up for lost time. He considered Melissa part of the package, of course.

"An invitation, of course," he said, wise enough to pacify Melissa. He wanted her in a receptive frame of mind tonight. He didn't want her stubborn streak kicking in. "Would you like to have dinner with me tonight at DiPasquali's?"

"I think your daughter is a little young for pizza."

Based on the spark of amusement in her eyes, she might have been teasing, but Cody took her comment seriously. He hadn't thought of that. In fact, what he really knew about babies would fit on the head of a pin. That was easily corrected. He would buy a book on parenting at the first opportunity. He was going to be the best-prepared father on the face of the planet, even if he was getting a late start.

"There must be something on the menu there she can eat," he said. "Or is there someplace that would be better?"

"DiPasquali's is fine," Melissa soothed. "I'll feed her first. She can chew on a slice of bread while we eat.

She'll be perfectly content. She loves to eat out. She gets a lot of attention.''

"Fine, whatever," he murmured distractedly, already thinking ahead to what he needed to accomplish between now and dinnertime.

He wanted to buy an engagement ring. And that book on parenting, of course. If he couldn't find one in town, maybe Luke or Jordan would have one he could borrow. He needed to call Lance Treethorn and tell him he wouldn't be returning to Wyoming. And he should sit down with his father and work out an arrangement for taking over his old duties at White Pines. Harlan would probably be relieved to be sharing the workload again.

"Cody?"

"Hmm?" He glanced up and caught Melissa's serious expression. "What's wrong?"

"Nothing. I'm just glad you want to be part of your daughter's life."

He stared at her, uncertain what would have made her ever suspect he'd do otherwise. "Well, of course, I do."

Melissa shrugged. "I wasn't sure how you were going to feel. And Mother, well, she had this crazy idea you were going to fight me for custody."

Cody couldn't imagine why he would have to fight for custody. He was going to claim his daughter *and* Melissa. If he'd known about the baby eighteen months ago, he would never have left for Wyoming in the first place. The incident with Brian might never have happened. He and Melissa would have been married.

Custody arrangements would never have become an issue. At least, he finally understood Velma's reaction to him.

"That explains why she's been looking at me as if I'm about to steal the silver," he said.

"Yes."

"Well, she can stop worrying. We'll settle everything tonight." He leaned down and dropped a kiss on Melissa's lips. "See you later."

"Settle everything?" she repeated, a note of anxiety in her voice. "Cody!"

He turned back.

"What does that mean, we're going to settle everything?"

He smiled. "Not to worry, darlin'. We'll talk about it tonight."

"Exactly what did he say?" Velma fretted as Melissa bathed her daughter and got her ready for their evening with Cody.

"He said we'd settle everything tonight." She grabbed Sharon Lynn's rubber duck in midair as her daughter hurled it from the tub.

"What does that mean?"

Melissa sighed. "I don't know what it means, Mother. I suppose I'll find out shortly."

"I don't like it. I think your father and I should be there to protect your interests."

"I doubt Cody intends to pluck Sharon Lynn out of her high chair at the restaurant and carry her off into the night," she said as she toweled her daughter dry.

"Anything other than that, I can cope with just fine on my own."

"What if he does decide to take her?"

"He won't," Melissa repeated, not sure how she knew with such conviction that Cody wouldn't do something so outrageous. "Stop worrying. I can handle Cody."

"You couldn't handle him two years ago," her mother commented. "What makes you think things are so different now?"

Melissa thought carefully about that before she answered. She used the struggle to get Sharon Lynn into her red corduroy pants and a cute little flowered shirt to buy some time.

"I'm stronger than I was then," she said eventually. "I've had almost two years to see that I don't need Cody Adams in order to survive. Sharon Lynn and I are doing just fine on our own."

Her mother regarded her skeptically. "Are you saying you're immune to him now?"

The kiss they'd shared on the front walk burned its way into her awareness. "No," she admitted. "I can't say that."

Velma groaned. "I knew it. I knew it the minute I saw the two of you playing kissy-face on the front walk."

"We were not playing kissy-face," Melissa retorted, blushing just the same. "Maybe you and Mabel have the same vocabulary after all."

"Mabel saw you kissing, too?"

"No, she just accused me of making goo-goo eyes at him way back in junior high."

"If only you'd limited yourself to that," Velma said dryly.

Melissa frowned. "If I had, we wouldn't have Sharon Lynn," she reminded her mother quietly.

Velma retreated into silence after that. She was still looking anxious when Cody arrived to pick them up. Melissa had a feeling she had her father to thank for keeping her mother from racing down the driveway after them. He appeared to have a tight grip on her elbow and a glint of determination in his eyes as he waved them off.

The ride to DiPasquali's took only minutes. It was a wonder they didn't crash into a tree, though. Cody couldn't seem to take his eyes off his daughter. Sharon Lynn returned his overt inspection with shy, little peek-a-boo smiles. Apparently she'd inherited her father's flirtatious nature, too, Melissa thought with some amusement. Cody was clearly captivated. She should have been pleased, but the doubts her mother had planted kept her from fully relaxing and enjoying the way father and daughter were bonding.

At the small Italian restaurant where both she and Cody were well known, they were ushered to a back booth amid exclamations over Sharon Lynn's outfit and Cody's return. Melissa didn't miss the speculative looks sent their way by customers who knew their history only too well.

Though a high chair was set up at the end of the table for the baby, Cody insisted she was just fine beside him in the booth. Sharon Lynn stood on the vinyl seat next to him, bouncing on tiptoes and patting Cody on the top of his head.

He circled her waist with his hands and lifted her into the air, earning giggles and a resounding kiss for his trouble. Melissa watched the pair of them with her heart in her throat. When Sharon Lynn climbed into Cody's lap, studied him seriously for a full minute, then cooed, "Da," Melissa felt the salty sting of tears in her eyes.

Cody's mouth dropped open. "Did she just call me Da?"

Apparently sensing approval, Sharon Lynn repeated the sound. "Da, Da, Da."

"She knows who I am," he whispered incredulously.

Melissa hated to disappoint him, but she knew that her daughter tended to call every man that. Besides, she refused to admit that she had tried to teach Sharon Lynn that very word while showing her a snapshot of Cody. She seriously doubted her daughter had actually made the connection between that blurry picture and the man holding her now.

She almost told him not to get too excited over it. Sharon Lynn might not even remember to connect that word with him tomorrow. The look in Cody's eyes kept her silent. He clearly wanted to believe that he and his child had made some sort of cosmic connection.

As she watched the pair of them, something shifted inside Melissa. Her earlier doubts fled. Maybe there really was some sort of instinctive bond between father and child. She wasn't sure what to make of this softer, gentler Cody. He had always been filled with laughter, but there was something incredibly sweet and tender in the way he teased his daughter and kept her giggling. Pride shone in his eyes at everything she did.

"She's brilliant," he declared every few minutes over the simplest accomplishments.

Sharon Lynn was clearly basking in the praise and the attention. Melissa held her breath, wondering just when exhaustion would overtake her daughter and turn that cheerful demeanor into far more familiar crankiness and tears. She couldn't help worrying about how Cody would respond to his child then. Would he turn tail and run again the instant the newness of this experience wore off, just as he had abandoned a long string of women once he'd tired of them? She was torn between anticipation and panic as she waited to see how the rest of the evening would play out.

They made it through their pizza without calamity striking. Sharon Lynn yawned a few times, grabbed a handful of the mushrooms Melissa had removed from her slice and squished them. When Cody tried to wipe her hands, she began sobbing as if she were being tortured.

Cody stared at Melissa helplessly as Sharon Lynn batted his hands away. "What did I do?"

"You didn't do anything. She's tired."

"Are you sure? Maybe she's hurt. Maybe there was a piece of glass and she cut herself." He unfolded her tightly clenched fingers and examined each one.

"Any sign of blood?" Melissa inquired, barely hiding her amusement.

He scowled at her. "How can you be so calm?"

"Because this is a nightly ritual."

He blanched. "Nightly?"

She nodded. "Just about. She gets so tired she can hardly keep her eyes open, but she doesn't want to miss anything, so she fights going to sleep."

Cody was regarding the sobbing child as if she were an alien creature. "Want me to take her?" she offered.

"No," he said insistently. "I have to learn how to deal with this."

He lifted Sharon Lynn up and sat her on the edge of the table facing him. Huge tears rolled down her blotchy cheeks. "Okay, kiddo, let's try to figure out a solution for this little problem you have with bedtime."

"Cody?"

He glanced up at her. "Hmm?"

"I don't think reason and logic are going to work."

"Sure they will," he argued. "Just watch."

He began talking in a low, soothing tone, explaining very patiently that sleep was very important. He added a lot of nonsense about fairy princesses and treasures that didn't come from any storybook Melissa had ever read.

Whether it was his tone or the actual words, Sharon Lynn's eyelids began to droop. The next thing Melissa knew, she was cradled in Cody's arms, sound asleep.

"Amazing," she admitted. "I should hire you to do that."

"No need to hire me," he said, his gaze suddenly fixed on her in a way that had her pulse scrambling. "I intend to be available for bedtime duty every night from now on."

Melissa swallowed hard against the tide of panic that swept through her. Surely she hadn't heard him right. "Excuse me?" she whispered.

"Once we're married, I'll get her to bed," he said, making his intentions perfectly clear.

"Married?" she repeated as if it were an unfamiliar concept.

"Well, of course," he said. "What did you think was going to happen?" He reached into his pocket, scooped something out and set it on the table between them.

Melissa stared at the small velvet box incredulously. She looked from it to Cody's face and back again.

"Go ahead," he encouraged. "Open it. If you'd rather have something else, we can go together tomorrow."

She shook her head, fighting the urge to grab that tempting little box and claim not only the ring inside, but the future Cody had obviously mapped out for them. This reaction of his to discovering he was a father wasn't even remotely what she had expected. Obviously he wasn't thinking clearly. He hadn't wanted to marry her two years ago. She was faintly insulted that it had taken a baby to drag a proposal out of him.

Actually, it wasn't even a proposal. It was another of those orders she hated so much. Issuing edicts was something he had learned at Harlan Adams's knee. Considering how he'd rebelled against his father, she would have thought he'd be more sensitive to the crummy habit.

"No," she said flatly, meeting his gaze evenly. She was very proud of herself for getting the word out, for keeping her voice and her resolve steady.

He blinked and stared. "No what?"

She drew in a deep breath and, before she could change her mind, blurted, "I will not touch that box and I will not marry you."

A red flush climbed up his neck. "Of course you will," he said just as emphatically. "Don't be stubborn, Melissa. It's the sensible thing to do."

"Sensible," she repeated in a low, lethal tone. "I do not intend to get married because it is *sensible!*"

She stood and jerked on her coat, then moved to pick up Sharon Lynn. Cody held his daughter out of her reach.

"Sit back down and let's talk about this," he ordered. "You're causing a scene."

"I don't care," she said emphatically, though she didn't dare look around to see just how many people were fascinated by their argument. "There is absolutely nothing to discuss."

"Please," he said, sounding slightly more meek.

Since when had Cody cared about scenes? Melissa regarded him suspiciously, but she did sit on the edge of the seat. She did not remove her coat.

"How about another soft drink?" he coaxed.

"Cody!"

"Okay, okay." He leaned toward her intently. "Maybe I didn't go about this quite right."

"I'll say."

He reached awkwardly around his sleeping daughter and picked up the velvet box. He flipped it open to display an impressive emerald surrounded by diamonds. Melissa fought to pretend that the ring didn't just about take her breath away. The size of the ring and the sparkle of those stones were not important. A marriage based on obligation was the real point here. She wouldn't have it.

"It reminded me of your eyes," Cody said. He grinned. "The way they are right now, when they're shooting off sparks."

Melissa's resolve wavered. A little voice in her head gathered steam, repeating *no, no, no* so loudly she couldn't ignore it. Hadn't she told herself just a few hours earlier that she'd always been too easy on Cody? Hadn't she made a fool of herself over and over again by giving in if he so much as smiled at her?

And hadn't she learned that she could take care of herself? She no longer liked the idea of relying on anyone, either financially or, even more importantly, for her happiness.

"You're wasting your time," she told him emphatically before her resolve could falter. "The ring is beautiful. You're a fine man. I'm thrilled that you want to be a part of Sharon Lynn's life. But I will not marry you."

He looked absolutely dumbfounded. If the conversation hadn't been quite so difficult for her, too, she might have smiled at his flabbergasted reaction.

"Why?" he demanded, staring at her, indignation radiating from every pore.

"Because I will not get married for all the wrong reasons."

"What wrong reasons? We have a child. I intend to be a father to her."

"That's fine. It doesn't mean you have to be a husband to me. I'm doing just fine on my own. You were apparently doing so fine on your own that you saw no need to come back for almost two years."

"That's it, isn't it?" His gaze narrowed. "You're just doing this to get even because I left town and you had to face being pregnant all alone."

Melissa regarded him sadly. "No, Cody, I am not trying to get even. I'm just trying not to compound one mistake by making another."

He seemed thoroughly taken aback by the realization that anyone—and most especially the woman who'd always adored him—would consider marrying him to be a mistake. Obviously his ego hadn't suffered any during their separation. It was as solid as ever.

She reached across the table and patted his hand. "It's nothing personal."

He stared at her. "How can you say that? I think it's pretty damned personal."

"Once you've had time to think it over, you'll see that I'm right," she assured him. "Obligation is a terrible basis for a marriage."

This time when she stood and reached for Sharon Lynn, he didn't resist. He pocketed the ring and stepped out of the booth. "I'll take you home," he said, his voice flat.

Melissa directed him to the small house she'd been renting for the past year, since about a month after Sharon Lynn's birth. Cody showed no inclination to get out of the pickup, so she let herself out. She hesitated for a moment with the door still open.

"I'm sorry, Cody. I really am."

He didn't look at her. "I'll call tomorrow and we'll work out a schedule for me to spend time with my daughter."

The chill in his voice cut straight through her. For the first time she wondered if she had made a terrible mistake in alienating him. Even though she knew in her heart that her decision was the right one, the only one to be made under the circumstances, perhaps she should have found a way to be more diplomatic about rejecting him.

"Fine," she said. "Whatever works for you will be okay."

She closed the door and started up the walk. An instant later she heard the engine shut off, then the slam of the driver's door behind Cody. He caught up with her before she could even make it to the front stoop.

Before she realized what he intended, he hauled her into his arms and kissed her so hard and so thoroughly that her head spun. Then, as if he suddenly became aware of the child she was holding or possibly because he figured he'd made his point, he released her.

"Give her to me," he said. "I'll carry her inside."

"Cody, she's fine," Melissa protested. She didn't want him inside, not when her knees were shaking and her pulse was racing.

"I said I'd carry her," he repeated, plucking her neatly out of Melissa's arms. "Open the door."

Following her directions, he made his way to the baby's small room. Angrily shrugging aside Melissa's offer of assistance, he fumbled with his daughter's clothes. He scanned the room, picked out a nightshirt from a small dresser, changed her, then laid her down gently.

Only then did a sigh shudder through him. His hand rested for a moment on the baby's backside.

"Good night, sweet pea," he murmured, his gaze riveted to his sleeping daughter as he backed toward the door.

The sight of Cody with their child, feeling his pain and his longing as he'd tucked her in for the night, had shaken Melissa. She was leaning against the wall outside the room, trying to gather her composure, when he finally emerged.

His gaze caught hers, burning into her. "It's not over," he said quietly. "Not by a long shot."

Trembling, Melissa stood rooted to the spot, staring after him long after she'd heard the truck's engine start, long after Cody had driven away.

Cody was right. It wasn't over. More than anything, she feared the struggle between them for their daughter was just beginning.

Chapter Seven

Cody didn't get a wink of sleep the entire night. When he wasn't overwhelmed by the amazing experience of holding his daughter, he was thinking about Melissa's astonishing transformation.

He had never noticed before how stubborn she was, nor how self-confident and independent. In fact, as he recalled, there had hardly ever been an occasion when she hadn't been thoroughly accommodating to his every whim. She'd picked a hell of a time to change, he thought, thoroughly disgruntled over having been shot down.

Sometime shortly after dawn, he finally forced himself to admit that he actually found the new Melissa ever so slightly more intriguing than he had the compliant woman he'd left behind.

Kelly, Jessie and the others had always warned him about taking Melissa for granted. It appeared he should have paid more attention to their advice. Melissa had used his time away to develop a very strong sense of who she was and what her priorities were. He was beginning to wonder if there really wasn't room for him in her life anymore.

Tired of his own company, he walked into the dining room at White Pines the minute he heard the rattle of breakfast dishes. Unfortunately, the housekeeper was very efficient. Maritza had already retreated to the kitchen, but she had left an array of cereals, a large pot of fresh coffee, a basket of warm rolls, and a bowl of berries, banana slices and melon. He noticed there were no eggs or bacon, no hash browns or grits. Obviously Harlan hadn't won his war to get what he considered to be a decent breakfast served during the week.

Cody was just pouring himself a cup of coffee when his father came in. He surreptitiously studied his father's face. Harlan looked tired and sad, but his complexion no longer had that unhealthy-looking pallor it had had when Cody had first arrived.

"You're up mighty early," Harlan observed, his expression sour as he surveyed the food the housekeeper had set out. "Dammit, I can't seem to get a decent piece of meat in the morning anymore." He shot a hopeful look at Cody. "Want to drive into town and get a real breakfast? Maybe a steak and some eggs?"

"And bring the wrath of Maritza down on my head? I don't think so. The fruit looks good."

"I don't see you eating any of it."

"I'm not hungry."

"Late night?"

"Something like that."

"I thought you were past carousing."

"Who was carousing? I had dinner with Melissa." He paused and drew in a deep breath. It was time to test the words on his lips, time to test his father's reaction. It would be a good barometer of what others would have to say.

"And my daughter," he added.

Harlan merely nodded, clearly not startled by the profound announcement.

"About time," he said succinctly.

Cody stared at him, his blood suddenly pumping furiously. "You knew, too? Dammit, Daddy, you're every bit as bad as Jordan," he accused. "You kept it from me, just like he did. What is wrong with everyone in this family? I thought we were supposed to stick together." He was just warming up to a really good tirade when his father cut in.

"Settle down, son. Nobody told me, if that's what you're thinking. Didn't take much to add up two and two, once I'd seen that child. She's the spitting image of you at that age. I've got a picture of you boys on my desk that would have reminded me, if I hadn't seen it for myself." He shrugged. "Besides, Melissa never had eyes for anyone but you."

Cody couldn't think of a thing to say. Apparently his father had been willing to stand on the sidelines and wait for Cody to show up and discover he had a daughter. It didn't fit with his usual manipulative style.

Either his father was mellowing or he had some other kind of devious scheme up his sleeve.

Harlan speared a chunk of cantaloupe, eyed it disparagingly, then ate it. "So," he began, his tone one of such studied indifference that Cody immediately went on alert. "Is that why you took off? Did Melissa tell you she was pregnant?"

Cody was horrified his father could think so little of him. Was that it? Had Harlan thought he'd already made his decision about marrying Melissa and being a father to his child?

"No, absolutely not," he declared indignantly. "Do you honestly think I have so little backbone that I'd run from a responsibility like that?"

His father shot a bland look in his direction. "I wouldn't like to think it, but the evidence was staring me in the face."

"What evidence?"

"You were gone. Your girl was pregnant. She quit college. She had to take that piddly job at Dolan's to make ends meet, which suggested that no one was paying a dime to support her or the baby. Didn't take a genius to add it all together and figure out that one."

"Well, your calculator malfunctioned this time," Cody snapped. "She never said a word, never even tried to track me down. The first I knew about that baby was when Velma Horton brought her into Dolan's when I was there the other day. Even then, I thought someone else had to be the father. It never crossed my mind that Melissa would hide something that important from me."

"I see." Harlan scooped up a strawberry, eyed it with disgust, then put it back. "Now that you know, what do you intend to do about it?"

"I proposed to her last night."

Harlan's eyes lit up. His expression was suddenly more animated than it had been in days. "Well, hell, son, why didn't you say so? Congratulations! When's the wedding?"

"No wedding," Cody admitted dully. "She said no."

Harlan's openmouthed expression of astonishment reflected Cody's feelings precisely.

"She flat-out turned you down?" his father said incredulously.

"Without so much as a hesitation," he said. "It was downright insulting."

Harlan chuckled. "Well, I'll be damned."

"You don't have to sound so amused," Cody grumbled.

"Sure, I do, boy. Seems tame little Melissa has grown up into a spirited young woman. The next few months or so ought to be downright interesting."

Cody glared at him. "Months? Forget it. I'm giving her a day, maybe two, to get over this contrariness. Then I'm hauling her to a justice of the peace."

His father started to laugh, then smothered the sound with a napkin. "Sorry," he mumbled, then gave up the fight and chuckled. "Son, you're going to be able to sell tickets to that one."

Cody's frayed temper snapped. He stood and tossed his own napkin back on the table. "Well, get out your checkbook, Daddy. The best seats in the house are going to cost you. Melissa and I might as well start off our married life with a nice little nest egg.''

Melissa wiped down the counter at Dolan's after the last of the lunch crowd had left and eyed Cody warily. He'd been skulking up and down the aisles of the drugstore since noon, but he hadn't come near the soda fountain. He seemed unaware that Eli and Mabel were watching him with overt fascination. Thankfully, he was also unaware of what his presence was doing to her pulse rate. Who knew what he would do to capitalize on that little hint of a fissure in her resolve.

''Mabel, why don't you take the rest of the afternoon off,'' Eli suggested, playing straight into Cody's hands.

''What's wrong with you, old man?'' Mabel grumbled. ''You planning on shutting down business?''

Eli gave her a pointed nod in Melissa's direction. ''Go on, Mabel. You've been wanting to check out the new seeds over at the hardware store so you can get your garden in at the first sign of spring. Go do it.''

Melissa almost chuckled as she watched Mabel struggle with herself. She'd been talking about those seeds for a week, ever since the hardware store owner had told her they'd arrived. She also hated to miss out on something with the kind of gossip potential that Melissa's next confrontation with Cody was likely to have.

''Go,'' Eli repeated, shooing her toward the door and taking the choice out of her hands. ''I might not feel so generous again anytime soon.''

"Don't doubt that," Mabel retorted sourly.

Mabel got her coat and left, reluctance written all over her narrow, tight-lipped face. Cody inched a little closer to the soda fountain, as if an invisible barrier had been removed from his path.

"Melissa," Eli called. "I'll be in the storeroom, checking this morning's delivery. Call me if you need me."

"Traitor," Melissa mumbled under her breath.

Cody had moved close enough by now to overhear. "Nice talk," he commented. "He's just doing you a favor."

"Me?" She stared at him incredulously. "Oh, no. You probably paid him to get rid of Mabel and to disappear himself. I noticed the other night that you'd inherited Harlan's knack for manipulation."

Cody clearly wasn't crazy about the comparison, but he let the charge roll off his back. "I'm not desperate enough to be paying anyone to give me time alone with you," Cody said, his grin widening. "I'm still relying on my charm."

"Take it somewhere else," she muttered.

"Tsk-tsk, Me...liss...a," he drawled, tipping his hat back on his head as he settled on a stool at the counter. "What does it take to get a little service around here?"

"More charm than you've got," she retorted. "Or cold, hard cash."

He plucked a twenty out of his wallet and set it on the counter. Then he winked. It appeared he was giving her a choice about which currency she wanted to accept. Melissa would have gladly taken the wink, if it meant she could shove that bill straight down his throat.

Since she couldn't, she snatched the twenty, tucked it into her pocket and withdrew her order pad and pen. "What'll it be?" she inquired in the same impersonal tone she used with other impossible customers.

Cody propped his elbows on the counter and leaned forward. "A kiss for starters."

"You wish." Her knees trembled despite the defiant retort. Why was it that temptation always entered a room right at Cody's side? Shouldn't she have been totally immune by now? Lord knows, she'd been lecturing herself on getting over him from the day he'd left town. Some of that advice should have taken by now. Apparently, though, it hadn't.

"Then I'll have a hamburger, fries and a shake," he said.

The mundane order was a disappointment. Melissa cursed her wayward hormones as she slapped the burger on the grill and lowered the fries into the hot grease. She sloshed milk into a metal container and out of habit added two scoops of chocolate ice cream, even though Cody hadn't specified the kind he wanted. Half of the mixture splashed out when she jammed the container into place on the automatic shaker.

"Nervous?" Cody inquired.

He spoke in a smug, lazy drawl that sent heat scampering down her spine. She scowled at him. "What on earth do I have to be nervous about? You're the one who doesn't belong here. You're the one making a pest of himself."

Sparks flared in his dark eyes. "Want me to ask Eli how he feels about you making a paying customer feel unwelcome?"

He didn't have to. She already knew that Eli would have heart failure if he heard her trying to run Cody off with her rudeness. He'd already taken Cody's side once today by slinking off to hide out in the storeroom to give them time alone. She'd never before noticed that Eli held Cody in particularly high esteem. His behavior must be part of some instinctive male support system that kicked in whenever one of them sensed that a woman might be getting the upper hand.

She turned her back on Cody, finished fixing his food, then set it down on the counter with a jarring thud.

He grinned at her. "Service with a smile," he commented. "I love it. You earn a lot of tips this way?"

Melissa closed her eyes and prayed for patience. When she opened them again, Cody hadn't vanished as she'd hoped. "Why are you in here?" she inquired testily. "Shouldn't you be out roping cattle or something?"

"We have plans to make, remember?"

"I told you just to tell me when you wanted to see Sharon Lynn. I'll make the arrangements so you can pick her up at my parents' anytime."

"Not those plans," he said complacently, picking a pickle off of his hamburger and tsk-tsking her, apparently for not remembering that he hated pickles.

"Sorry," she said without much sincerity. She should have dumped in the whole damned jar. "You could have eaten at Rosa's."

"I prefer the spice here," he retorted. "Now let's get back to those plans. I was thinking that a week from Saturday would be good."

Melissa was surprised he wanted to wait that long before seeing his daughter again. Maybe his fascination was already waning. At this rate he'd be moving back to Wyoming in a month. Surely she could wait him out that long. She'd probably be a tangled heap of frustrated hormones, but presumably her sanity would still be intact.

"Sure, if that's what you want," she said more agreeably now that she knew he was likely to be out of her hair in no time. "I'm off on Saturday, so you can pick Sharon Lynn up at my place."

"Not just Sharon Lynn," he corrected. "Can't have a wedding without the bride."

Melissa dropped the glass she'd been rinsing out. It shattered at her feet. Eli poked his head out of the storeroom, saw the glass and shook his head.

"I hope to hell you two settle this quick," the pharmacist said. "It's costing me a fortune in broken glasses."

"Don't worry, Eli," Cody consoled him. "I'll settle up with you." He fixed his unrelenting gaze on Melissa and added, "I always accept my responsibilities."

"Oh, stuff a rag in it," Melissa retorted, stripping off her apron and opening the cash register to shove in the twenty she'd pocketed. "Eli, I'm leaving. Mr. Adams has already paid his check. Keep the change."

She made it as far as the sidewalk, still shrugging into her coat, when Cody caught up with her. If her refusal to kowtow to his wishes for a second time had ruffled his feathers, he wasn't letting it show. He fell into step beside her, his expression perfectly innocent.

"Going to pick up the baby?"

Actually Melissa had no idea where she was going. She'd been so anxious to get away from Cody that she'd walked out of the drugstore without the kind of plan she should have had. It was an unfortunate sign of weakness, one she couldn't allow him to detect.

"No, actually, I have things to do."

"Like what? I'll help."

"No, thanks. I can handle it."

"Come on, Me...liss...a," he coaxed, planting himself on the sidewalk in front of her, legs spread. He rocked back on the heels of his cowboy boots and peered at her from beneath the brim of his hat. It was a look that invited a woman to swoon. She ought to know. She'd done it often enough, flat-out making a fool of herself over him.

"Would spending a little time with me be so awful?" he inquired.

Awful? That wasn't the word she would have chosen. Dangerous, maybe. Stupid. Risky. There was a whole string of applicable words and none of them had anything to do with awful.

"I'd rather not," she said politely.

"Bet I can change your mind," he countered, grinning at her.

She scowled at him as he advanced on her step by step. "Don't try."

He shook his head. "I don't know. The temptation is pretty great. Your mouth is all pouty. Very kissable," he assessed, his gaze hot on her. He took yet another step closer, crowding her. "Your cheeks are pink. Just about the color of rose petals and twice as soft. It's all hard to resist."

As he spoke, her lips burned as if he'd kissed them. Her cheeks flamed, turning to what she was sure must be a deeper shade. Damn, it didn't seem to matter if he actually touched her or not. Her body reacted predictably just to the provocative suggestion.

"Go away," she ordered in a voice that was entirely too breathless.

His expression solemn, he shook his head. "I can't do that, Me . . . liss . . . a."

She sighed. "Why not?" she demanded far too plaintively.

He circled one arm around her waist and dragged her against him. She could feel the hard heat of his arousal.

"You know the answer to that," he whispered, his lips scant millimeters from hers. His breath fanned across her cheek.

"Cody." His name came out as a broken sigh, a protest that not even someone far less relentless than Cody would have heeded.

"It's okay," he consoled her. "Everything is going to turn out just fine."

He slanted his mouth over hers then, setting off fireworks in January. *Why, why, why?* her brain demanded. Why was her body so darned traitorous? Maybe it was like the tides. Maybe the way she responded to Cody was as immutable as the sun setting in the west.

She resisted the explanation. It meant she had no will at all to fight it. She put her hands on his chest and shoved with all her might. She might as well have been trying to topple a centuries' old oak. Cody didn't budge. He didn't stop that tender assault on her mouth.

For what seemed an eternity he coaxed and plundered, teased and tasted until she was shivering with urgent and almost-forgotten need. When she was weak with a desire she definitely didn't want to feel, Cody finally released her. She very nearly melted at his feet. In fact, she might have if he hadn't kept his hands resting possessively on her hips. Even through her coat, her skin burned at his touch.

"So, what are we going to do with the rest of the afternoon?" he inquired. The gleam in his eyes suggested he had an idea of his own. His lips quirked up in the beginnings of a smile.

"Not what you're thinking," she said curtly.

His grin spread. "Don't be so certain of that, sweet pea. It sounds an awful lot like a challenge and you know I never could resist a dare."

Desperate for space, she backed away from him. "Give it a rest," she said crankily.

He reached out and rubbed his thumb across her lower lip. The sensation sent fire dancing through her.

"I'm just getting started, darlin'," he murmured, his gaze locked with hers.

Melissa held back a sigh of resignation. "You're not going home, are you?"

"When I can be with you? No way."

"Come on, then."

His expression immediately brightened. Once more he fell dutifully into step beside her. "Where are we going?"

"To buy groceries," she said, plucking a boring chore out of thin air. "And after that, we're ironing." She slanted a look at him to judge his reaction. He didn't bat an eye.

"Sounds downright fascinating," he declared. He captured her gaze, then added slowly, "I've always been particularly fond of starch."

She ignored the provocative tone. "Oh, really?" she said skeptically.

"Yes, indeed," he swore. "In my shirts and in my women. And you, sweet pea, are full of it."

Melissa had a feeling it would take her weeks to puzzle out whether he meant that as a compliment. For the first time, though, she had this funny little feeling she was going to have the time of her life figuring it out.

Chapter Eight

Somewhere in the middle of the grocery store, Melissa lost track of Cody. She was aware of the precise instant when she no longer felt the heat of his stare or the sizzling tension of his nearness. She almost sagged with relief, even as she fought off a vague stirring of disappointment. Clearly his attention span was no better now than it had ever been.

Worse, he was getting to her. Despite her best intentions, she was responding to his teasing, to the allure of his body. She could not let that happen. Steering totally clear of him, however, seemed to be the only way she was likely to be able to avoid succumbing to that seductive appeal. Now seemed like a good time to make a break for it.

All she had to do was get through the checkout line and race home before he caught up with her. She could barricade the door. Or maybe just hide out in a bedroom until he was convinced she wasn't home.

She tossed a six-pack of soft drinks she didn't need into the cart, just in case Cody wasn't as far away as she hoped. She had to leave the store with more than a quart of milk or he'd know that this trip had been nothing more than a ploy to avoid being alone with him.

She had rounded the last aisle and was heading for the cashier when she spotted him. He was positioned in front of the baby food, studying labels with the intensity of a scientist in his lab. Apparently, though, he wasn't so absorbed that her presence escaped his notice.

"Which of these does Sharon Lynn like?" he asked, holding up competing brands of strained peas.

"Neither one."

His brow knit worriedly. "Doesn't she have to eat vegetables?"

"Yes, but she's past the baby food. She has her first baby teeth. She can chew soft food." She regarded him oddly. "Do you really care about this?"

"Yes," he said succinctly, and replaced the peas. "Fill me in on everything."

Melissa shrugged. "Okay. She can eat the junior brands. Like these," she said, plucking a couple of jars off the shelf. "There are some foods that don't have to be specially prepared. She can eat the regular stuff. Peas, for example."

To her surprise, he seemed to be taking in every word as if she were delivering a fascinating treatise on something far more significant than baby food. In the past he'd reserved that kind of attention for very little besides ranching.

"What are her favorite foods?" he asked, studying the larger jars intently.

"Ice cream and French fries."

Cody stared at her. "That's her diet?"

"No," she said patiently. "Those are her favorites." She gestured to the junior baby food. "This is what she gets most of the time. When I have time, I even blend some myself from fresh fruits and vegetables. She's particularly fond of squishing bananas."

Cody eyed the jars of carrots and meats and fruits, seemed to struggle with his conscience, and then turned his back on them. "Let's go."

"Where?"

"To the ice cream section," he said as grimly as if he were going into battle and the enemy had pulled a last-minute tactical switch. "I'm not bringing home jars of that disgusting-looking liver or those limp little bits of carrot if she'd rather have ice cream."

"Cody, I do feed her. You don't need to stock my refrigerator, especially not with ice cream."

He stopped in his tracks and turned to face her. "Don't you see, this isn't about you. It's about me and my daughter. You've had her to yourself for thirteen months. Now I want a chance to be important in her life."

"By stuffing her with chocolate-fudge ice cream?"

Instead of taking her well-intended point, he seized on the tiny sliver of information she'd imparted about their daughter. "Is that her favorite? I'll buy a gallon of it."

He sounded relieved to know that he wouldn't have to resort to another round of guesswork and label-reading. In fact, he was loping off to the frozen food section before Melissa could gather her thoughts sufficiently to argue with him.

Okay, she told herself, it was only a gallon of ice cream. So what? It wasn't as if he could buy their daughter's affection or ruin her health with one extravagant gesture of chocolate fudge.

She had a feeling, though, that this was only the beginning. Cody was not a man to do anything by half measures. His retreat to Wyoming, abandoning not only her but his beloved home and family, was a perfect example of that. He could have straightened everything out between them with a few questions or even by hurling accusations and listening to explanations. Instead he had leapt to a conclusion and reacted by impetuously fleeing to another state.

He was doing much the same thing now that he had discovered he had a daughter. He wanted to be in her life—completely—right this instant. He wanted to marry Melissa...right this minute. The concepts of moderation or patience had obviously escaped him.

She sighed as he appropriated the shopping cart. The two half gallons of chocolate-fudge ice cream had turned into four. And she didn't like the gleam in his eyes one bit as he turned the cart on two wheels and headed straight for the shelves of diapers.

She'd been right. He was going to take over and she had a sinking feeling in the pit of her stomach that there would be very little she could do about it.

Cody realized he had almost lost it there for a minute at the supermarket. He'd wanted to sweep entire shelves of baby food into the shopping cart.

As it was, in addition to the ice cream, they had left the store with five, giant economy-size packages of disposable diapers, a new toy duck for Sharon Lynn's bath, five storybooks he could read to her at bedtime and an astonishing selection of her favorite juices. Melissa had just rolled her eyes at the startled checkout clerk.

"New father?" the girl had guessed.

"New enough," Melissa had replied.

Let them make fun, Cody thought. He didn't care. This was the first step in his campaign to make himself indispensable to Melissa and his daughter.

"Where to now?" he asked when they'd piled all those diapers and the rest of the shopping bags into the back of his pickup.

"I'm going home to iron," Melissa said, sticking to that absurd story she'd told him earlier in a blatant attempt to get rid of him. "Unless, of course, you'd like to do it for me?"

He frowned at her. "What about Sharon Lynn?"

"She's with Mother."

"I'll drop you off and go get her," he suggested eagerly.

"She's probably still taking her nap," Melissa said.

She said it in such a rush he had the feeling she thought he intended to kidnap the baby and take off with her. As much as he resented the implication, he kept his tone perfectly even. "She won't sleep forever," he countered reasonably. "I'll bring her straight home. I promise."

"You don't have a car seat," she noted pointedly.

Damn, but there was a lot to remember. "We'll stop now and get one."

"All of that ice cream will melt."

He frowned at the obstacles she kept throwing in his path. "Not in this weather. It's freezing out. And if it does, I'll buy more."

"Couldn't you just drop me off at home?"

"No, you need to come with me. You can show me the best kind of car seat."

Melissa sighed heavily. "Cody, what's the point? They're expensive and you probably won't . . ."

He guessed where she was going. "Won't what? Won't be here long enough to use it? You can get that idea right out of your head."

He tucked a finger under her chin and forced her to face him. "I've quit my job in Wyoming. I am home to stay, Melissa. Get used to it."

She held up her hands. "Sorry. I didn't mean anything. I was just trying to keep you from wasting money."

"If it's for my daughter, it is not a waste of money," he said curtly. "Now, can I find the kind of car seat I need at the discount superstore out on the highway?"

She nodded.

He turned the truck around on a dime, spewing gravel. He drove ten miles before his temper had cooled enough to speak again. He'd set out today to woo Melissa into changing her mind about marrying him. His first overtures, however, appeared to have gone awry. He'd lost his sense of humor, right along with his temper. It was no way for the two of them to start over. He sucked in a deep breath and made up his mind to mend fences.

"Truce?" he suggested, glancing over at her. She was huddled against the door, looking miserable. She shrugged.

"I'm not an ogre," he stated. "I'm just trying to fit into Sharon Lynn's life." Her gaze lifted to meet his. "And yours."

She sighed. "We don't need you," she repeated stubbornly. "We were doing just fine before you came back."

He ignored the tide of hurt that washed through him at the dismissive comment. "Maybe I need you."

Melissa frowned. "Yeah, right," she said sarcastically. "As if Cody Adams ever needed anybody. Didn't you pride yourself on staying footloose and fancy free?"

He saw no point in denying something she knew better than anyone. "I did," he agreed. He thought about the agonizing loneliness of that cabin he'd sentenced himself to in Wyoming. "Maybe being alone for the past eighteen months has changed me. Maybe I'm not the selfish, carefree, independent cuss who stormed away from Texas."

"And maybe pigs can fly," she countered.

He grinned at her. "Maybe they can," he said quietly. "If you believe in magic."

"I don't," she said succinctly.

Cody heard the terrible pain in her voice, even if her expression remained absolutely stoic. Dear heaven, what had he done to her by running off and leaving her to face being pregnant all alone? He saw now what he hadn't observed before. Not only was Melissa stronger and more self-sufficient, she also had an edge of cynicism and bitterness that hadn't been there before. The blame for that was his, no one else's.

At the discount store, when Melissa would have grabbed the first car seat they came across, Cody stopped her, deliberately taking the time to read the package for every last detail on safety. If nothing else, he intended to impress on Melissa that he took his parenting responsibilities seriously. Nothing was too trivial, too expensive, or too complicated to tackle if it had to do with his daughter.

Nearly an hour later they finally loaded the new car seat into the truck.

"I think that salesclerk despaired of ever getting you to make a choice," Melissa said, the beginnings of a smile tugging at her lips.

"It wasn't for her kid," he retorted.

"Okay, forget the salesclerk. Should I point out that the one you ended up taking is exactly the same one I tried to get you to buy when we walked in?"

He scowled at her. "What's your point?"

"That I had already done the exact same research, reached the exact same conclusion. You insisted I come along because you claimed to want my advice. When it came right down to it, though, you didn't trust me."

Cody carefully considered the accusation before turning to meet her gaze. "You're right. I should have listened to you. It's just that this is new to me. I'm trying to get it right. I don't want to mess up with something this important."

Her expression softened. "Cody, I can understand that. Really, I can. I was just as obsessive when I first brought Sharon Lynn home from the hospital. Mother and Daddy thought I was a lunatic. I didn't trust a piece of advice they offered. I was convinced it was probably outdated. I had to do it all for myself. Talk about reinventing the wheel." She shook her head. "I wasted more time, only to find myself doing exactly what they'd suggested in the first place."

He grinned. "You're just trying to save me traveling over the same learning curve, is that it?"

"Exactly," she said. She reached over and patted his hand. "I'm not trying to keep you out of Sharon Lynn's life, or control your input, or anything like that. I promise."

The impulsive touch didn't last nearly long enough. Cody grabbed her hand and pulled it to his lips. He brushed a kiss across her knuckles and saw the instantaneous spark of desire in her eyes. "I'll try to watch the defensiveness, if you'll do something for me."

She regarded him with conditioned wariness. "What?"

"Bring Sharon Lynn out to White Pines this weekend," he coaxed persuasively. At the flare of panic in her eyes, he pulled out his strongest ammunition—her fondness for Harlan. "I think seeing her would do Daddy a world of good. With Mother gone, he needs something positive in his life, something to cheer him up. You should have seen the look in his eyes this morning when I told him she was mine."

The hint of wariness in her eyes fled and was promptly replaced by astonishment. "You told him?"

"I did. But it wasn't news. He'd figured it out the first time he saw her, the same as Jordan had."

Her mouth gaped. "And he didn't do anything about it? I'm amazed he didn't haul your butt straight back here or offer to set up a trust fund for the baby or something."

"Frankly, so am I. Maybe he's learned his lesson about manipulating."

Melissa's expression was every bit as skeptical as his own had to be. "Okay," he said. "He probably has a scheme we don't know about yet. Even so, are you willing to take a chance? Will you bring her out? It's time she learned something about her father's side of the family."

He was playing to her sense of fairness and it was clearly working. He could practically read her struggle with her conscience on her face.

"I'll bring her," Melissa finally agreed with obvious reluctance. "On one condition—no tricks."

Cody regarded her innocently. Now that he'd gotten her basic agreement, he could go along with almost anything she demanded. "What kind of tricks?"

"No preachers lurking in the shadows. No wedding license all signed and ready to be filled in."

He feigned astonishment, even though he thought she might actually have a very good idea, one that hadn't even occurred to him until just that minute. "Would I do that?"

"In a heartbeat," she said. "And even if you had an attack of conscience, Harlan wouldn't. No conspiracies, okay?"

"Cross my heart," Cody said, already wondering if there was some way to pull off such a wedding.

Melissa's gaze narrowed. "Why doesn't that reassure me?"

"And you accused me of a lack of trust," he chided.

"I'm not the one whose brother threw a surprise wedding in place of a rehearsal," she said, reminding him of the sneaky trick Jordan and Kelly had pulled on his parents to avoid the out-of-control celebration his mother had planned for their wedding. The whole town had gossiped about that little stunt for weeks.

"I'm glad you mentioned that," Cody taunted. "It does give me some interesting ideas."

"Cody Adams, I am warning you . . ."

"No need, sweet pea. I'm not fool enough to take a chance on getting rejected in front of my family and the preacher. When you and I get married, it'll be because you're willing and eager.''

"'When,' not 'if'?" she chided.

"That's right, darlin'. Only the timing is left to be decided,'' he declared with far more confidence than he felt. He unloaded the last of their packages under Melissa's irritated scrutiny. Apparently, though, his certainty about their future had left her speechless. He considered that a hopeful sign.

"See you on Saturday,'' he said, escaping before he had a chance to put his foot in his mouth. "Come on out about eight. You can have breakfast with us.''

Besides, he thought, if Melissa was there by eight, that gave him most of the day to convince her to have a wedding at sunset.

Melissa debated bailing out on her day at White Pines. Handling Cody was tricky enough without having to worry about Harlan's sneaky tactics at the same time. Still, she couldn't very well deny Harlan the chance to get to know the granddaughter he'd just officially discovered he had.

That was what ultimately decided her, or so she told herself as she dressed Sharon Lynn in bright blue corduroy pants, a blue and yellow shirt, and tiny sneakers. She brushed her hair into a halo of soft curls around her face.

"Ma? Bye-bye?''

Proud of Sharon Lynn's expanding vocabulary, she nodded. "That's right, my darling. We're going to see your daddy and your granddaddy.''

Sharon Lynn's face lit up. She reached for the new toy duck that was never far from sight. "Da?"

Melissa shook her head at the instant reaction. Obviously Cody had had an incredible impact on his daughter in just one visit. Did he have that effect on all women or just those in her family? She tickled Sharon Lynn until she dissolved into a fit of giggles.

"Yes, Da," she told her approvingly. "We're going to see Da." And she, for one, was nervous as the dickens about it. Sharon Lynn clearly had no such qualms.

When Melissa pulled her car to a stop in front of the house at White Pines, she drew in a deep, reassuring breath, trying to calm her jitters. It was going to be just fine, she told herself, even as she fought the overwhelming sense of déjà vu that assailed her.

How many times had she driven out here, filled with hope, anxious to spend time with the man she loved, only to leave bitterly disappointed by his refusal to commit to anything more than a carefree relationship? Everything had always seemed more intense out here, the air crisper and cleaner, the terrain more rugged, the colors brighter. Similarly, her emotions had always seemed sharper, too—the bitter sorrow as well as the blinding joy.

Once she had dreamed of this being her home, the place where she and Cody would raise a family. Now with the snap of her fingers and a couple of "I do's," her dream could come true. But Cody's proposal, forced only by the existence of a child for whom he felt responsible, had tarnished the dream. She doubted it could ever recapture its original, innocent glow.

"Da, Da, Da!" Sharon Lynn screamed excitedly, bouncing in her car seat as Cody strode across the front lawn. He was wearing snug, faded jeans, a T-shirt that hugged his broad chest and worn cowboy boots. He looked sexier and more masculine than any male model ever had in *GQ*.

Before Melissa could fight her instinctive reaction just to the sight of him, he had thrown open the door and lifted his daughter high in the air, earning squeals of delight for his effort.

"Hey, pumpkin, I could hear you all the way inside the house," he teased the baby. "Your grandpa Harlan said you were loud enough to wake half the county. He's thinking of getting you geared up for the hog-calling contest at the state fair. What do you think?"

Melissa noted he reported his father's reaction with unmistakable pride. He glanced her way just then and the humor in his eyes darkened to something else, something she recognized from times past as powerful, compelling desire. Whatever was behind his proposal of marriage, the one thing she couldn't doubt was Cody's passion. He wanted her and he was doing nothing to hide that fact from her.

"Thank you for coming," he said, his expression solemn.

"I told you I would."

He shrugged. "You never know, though. Sometimes things come up."

Suddenly, for the first time Melissa was able to pinpoint the most devastating problem between them.

Neither of them had so much as a shred of trust left for the other.

She didn't trust Cody not to leave again. She didn't trust him not to rip her daughter away from her.

And worse, to her way of thinking because she knew he had a right to feel as he did, he didn't trust her to keep her promises. She had kept the secret of his daughter from him. He had to wonder if he could trust her to be honest with him about anything.

All at once she was unbearably sad. Regrets for the open, honest relationship they had once shared tumbled through her, leaving her shaken.

Before she realized he'd even moved, Cody was beside her, Sharon Lynn in his arms.

"Are you okay?" he asked, his expression filled with concern.

"Of course. Why would you think I wasn't?"

"Maybe it has something to do with the tears."

She hadn't even realized she was crying. She brushed impatiently at the telltale traces. "Sorry."

"You don't have to apologize, for heaven's sake. Just tell me what's wrong."

"An attack of nostalgia," she said, knowing it was only partially true. "Nothing to worry about." She plastered a smile on her face. "Come on. Let's go inside before Harlan falls out of that window he's peeking through."

Almost as if he'd heard the comment, the curtains fell back into place and a shadow moved away from the downstairs window. Cody grinned at her.

"He can't wait to meet Sharon Lynn. If you think I'm bad, wait until you see the room he's fixed up for her visits."

The implications of the lighthearted remark sent panic racing through Melissa. If Harlan had fixed up a room, then he clearly intended for Sharon Lynn to be at White Pines a lot. Was this visit just a prelude to the custody battle her mother had warned her about? Cody might not be willing to fight her in court, but Harlan was another matter. With Mary dead and his life stretching out emptily in front of him, who could tell what kind of crazy notion he might get into his head.

Apparently her fears must have been written on her face, because Cody halted again. "Melissa, you don't have to worry," he reassured her. "It's just a room. You know Harlan. Everything drives him to excess."

"You're sure that's all it is?"

"Very sure. You don't have anything to worry about from Harlan." That said, he winked at her. "I, however, am another matter entirely. I've given up on winning you with diapers and juice and toys."

"Oh?"

"I intend to win you with my sexy, wicked ways."

He was up the front steps and in the house before she had a chance to react. When she could finally move again, her legs wobbled and her pulse was scampering crazily.

Suddenly any threat Harlan might pose dimmed in importance. Cody was the one she needed to worry about. Always had been. Always would be.

Chapter Nine

At the precise instant that Cody and Melissa entered the front door at White Pines, Harlan stepped into the foyer. His prompt presence indicated that he had indeed been watching for Melissa's arrival and was eager for an introduction to his granddaughter.

Cody studied his father's face closely as Harlan's gaze honed in immediately on Sharon Lynn. For the first time since the funeral, there was a spark of animation in his dark eyes. And when he glanced at Melissa that animation included her, only to be quickly replaced by questions, unanswerable questions Cody hoped he wouldn't get into right off.

To stave them off, Cody crossed the wide sweep of wood floor and woven Mexican rug to stand in front of his father, Sharon Lynn still perched in his arms.

"Daddy, meet your granddaughter, Sharon Lynn."

The baby responded to the cue as if she'd been coached. A dimpled smile spread across her face as she held out her arms to be transferred to her new grandfather's embrace. Harlan accepted her with alacrity.

"You are a mighty fine young lady," he told her, his expression sober, his eyes unmistakably welling up with rare tears. "I'm very glad to be welcoming you to the family." His gaze shifted then to encompass Melissa once more. "It's good to see you again, girl. We've missed you around here."

Cody saw the sheen of tears spring to Melissa's eyes and realized more than ever what he had cost them all by running off as he had. His parents had always accepted that Melissa would one day be his wife. They had approved of her spirit, her kindness and her unconditional love for him. Melissa had been present on most family occasions, welcomed as if their relationship had been sealed.

Though he'd never asked his parents if they had continued to see her, he had suspected Melissa wouldn't feel that same sense of belonging after he'd gone. He knew from his father's comment just now that she had indeed stayed away and that her absence had hurt them all, costing them a relationship they held dear. The severing of ties had been as complete as if he and Melissa had been married and then divorced in an incredibly acrimonious manner that had forced everyone to choose sides.

"Thank you, Harlan," she said, stepping closer to be enveloped in a fierce hug that included Sharon

Lynn. "I've missed you, too. And I'm so terribly, terribly sorry about Mary."

"I know you are. Mary thought a lot of you, girl. She always hoped..." At a warning glance from Cody, he allowed his voice to trail off, the thought left unspoken.

It hardly mattered, though. The damage had already been done. Melissa's cheeks turned bright pink. Cody could feel the blood climbing up the back of his neck, as well. His father surveyed them both, then gave a brief nod of satisfaction as if he'd learned something he'd hoped for.

"Come on, then," Harlan said, his voice laced with a telltale trace of huskiness. "Let's go have some breakfast, before we all turn maudlin and start bawling."

To Cody's relief, his father left the subject of the past untouched beyond that single, oblique reference. Either he was far too fascinated by the child he held or he recognized that it was not a conversation to be held in the baby's presence.

There was no mistaking, though, that more questions lingered in his eyes. Cody guessed they would be as much about the future as the past. He also knew there were no answers his father would like hearing, not yet anyway. Harlan had the same impatience as his sons. He liked things settled to his satisfaction. Between Cody and Melissa nothing was settled at all.

Sharon Lynn patted her grandfather's face, then glanced to her mother for approval. "Da?" she questioned.

Cody scowled as he realized that he wasn't unique in his daughter's view. He caught Melissa's grin and realized how pitiful it was to be jealous of his own father.

Unaware, as Cody had been, that it was Sharon Lynn's universal name for any adult male, Harlan beamed at her. "Damn, but you're a smart one," he praised. "You and I need to have ourselves a little talk. What other words do you know?"

"Ma and bye-bye," Melissa offered. "It limits the conversations tremendously."

Cody noticed that his father didn't seem to mind. He seemed perfectly content to carry on a one-sided conversation with his granddaughter. It was probably the first time in years someone hadn't talked back to him.

The distraction also kept Harlan from touching the eggs and bacon he normally couldn't wait to eat on the weekends. Possibly that was the most telling indication of all of Sharon Lynn's power over this new male in her life.

"So, Sharon Lynn, have you ever seen a horse?" Harlan inquired.

Cody chuckled as his daughter tilted her head, a quizzical expression on her face as she appeared to give the question serious consideration.

"I'll take that for a no," Harlan said. "In that case, I think it's about time to fix that. Can't have a rancher's baby who doesn't know about horses. Maybe we'll even go for a little ride."

Cody glanced at Melissa to check her reaction to the instantaneous bonding between Sharon Lynn and his father. To his astonishment, the color had drained out of her face. Clearly the idea of Sharon Lynn going off with Harlan panicked her in some way. What he couldn't figure was why.

"Harlan, I really don't think—" she began.

"Don't worry about a thing," Harlan reassured her, cutting off her words. "I had every one of my boys up on horseback when they were no bigger than this. She'll fit right on the saddle in front of me. She'll be just fine. I guarantee I won't let her tumble off."

Harlan and the baby were out the door before Melissa could offer the firmer protest that was clearly on the tip of her tongue. Cody knew better than to argue with Harlan. He also knew that Sharon Lynn would be perfectly safe with his father. However, he could see that Melissa wouldn't believe it unless she witnessed their adventure on horseback with her own eyes. He put down his fork.

"Come on," he said. "You'll be worrying yourself sick, if you're not right alongside them."

"She's too little to be riding a horse," Melissa complained, her complexion still pale as she followed him outside. "She'll be terrified."

"I doubt that," Cody said. "You're projecting your feelings onto her. You never were much for horses. I guess you were more of a city girl than I realized."

She shot him a wry look. "Hardly that."

He grinned at her. "I don't know. About the only time I could get you into the barn was when I wanted to tumble you into the haystack."

"Cody Adams, that is not true," she contradicted, patches of bright color flaring in her cheeks. "Besides, that has absolutely nothing to do with Sharon Lynn and this crazy idea Harlan has of getting onto a horse with her."

"Stop fussing. She's just the right age to be introduced to riding. Kids her age have no fear. It's not like Daddy's going to put her on the horse, hit its rump and send her galloping around the paddock. He's going to be in the saddle, holding her."

"I suppose," Melissa said, but her gaze immediately sought out some sign of Sharon Lynn the minute the barn came into view.

The little cutie was hard to miss. She was squealing with delight from her perch atop the fence around the paddock. Misty, the oldest, smallest and gentlest of their mares, had come to investigate. Sharon Lynn's eyes were wide with excitement as she patted the white blaze on Misty's head.

"This is Misty," Harlan was explaining quietly, his grip firm on the horse's bridle. "Can you say that? Misty."

"Mi'ty," Sharon Lynn dutifully repeated, surprising all of them.

The horse neighed softly at hearing her name.

Cody glanced at Melissa and saw that she'd finally begun to relax. Her gaze was riveted on her daughter, though. He sensed that if Misty so much as shied back a step, Melissa was poised to snatch Sharon Lynn out of harm's way.

Just when he thought the worst of her reaction was past, she turned and looked up at him, anxiety and dismay clearly written all over her face. "How can your father even think about getting on a horse ever again?" she asked in a low voice, not meant to carry.

As if he'd been struck by a bolt of lightning, Cody finally realized why Melissa had been so upset by Harlan introducing Sharon Lynn to riding. The accident that had cost his mother her life hadn't even crossed his mind when Harlan had suggested bringing Sharon Lynn out to see the horses. But obviously the way Mary Adams had died had left an indelible image on Melissa's mind, as it might on anyone who didn't have the sensitivity of a slug, Cody chided himself. She had been fearful of horses to begin with. His mother's death could only have exaggerated that fear.

"Damn, no wonder you turned white as a sheet a minute ago when Daddy suggested bringing Sharon Lynn out here," he apologized. "You were thinking about what happened to Mother, weren't you?"

"Aren't you?" she asked, staring at him incredulously.

"No," he said honestly. "There's no point in blaming the horse for what happened to Mother. It was an accident and not an uncommon one at that. The horse was spooked by a snake. Even then, the fall might not have killed her. It was the way she landed."

Melissa shuddered. "Still, how can either one of you not think about it every single time you see a horse?"

"Because Daddy is a rancher, through and through. So am I," Cody said, trying to explain to Melissa what must seem inexplicable. "There are some things over which a rancher has no control. Rattlers spooking a horse is one of them."

He glanced at his father. "If he blames anyone or anything for what happened to Mother, it's more than likely himself for suggesting that ride in the first place. He also knows that the only way to conquer the fear after what happened is to get right back on a horse. He's been out riding over that same stretch of land every single day since she died."

Melissa clearly wasn't reassured. "I don't care about conquering fear. All I see is that your mother's death should be a damn good reason for him not to bring his granddaughter anywhere near a horse," she argued. "She's a baby, Cody."

Cody was beginning to see there was no reasoning with her on this. It was too soon after his mother's tragic accident. "If it's really upsetting you, I'll talk him out of it," he offered. "But sooner or later, Sharon Lynn will ride. She can't have a cowboy for a daddy and not learn."

Melissa rested her hand on his forearm. The expression on her face pleaded with him.

"Later, please," she said. "Just the thought of it after what happened to your mom makes me sick."

Cody could see that she wasn't exaggerating. Though he didn't agree with her, he could feel some compassion for the anxiety she was experiencing. He walked over and spoke to his father. Harlan shot a look over his shoulder at Melissa and gave an understanding nod.

"Of course," he apologized at once. "I didn't realize it would bother her so."

"Neither did I," Cody said. "But she's practically turning green."

"You take this little angel on inside, then. I'll be there in a bit."

Cody reached for his daughter, who let out a scream the instant she realized she was being taken away from the horse.

"Mi'ty!" she sobbed plaintively. "Mi'ty!"

"You'll see Misty another time," Cody promised. "Right now, I'm going to take you inside so you can see all of your new toys that Granddaddy bought you."

He wasn't sure if Sharon Lynn totally understood exactly what having Harlan Adams as a benefactor was all about until they reached the room he'd filled with everything from a set of white baby furniture with pink gingham sheets and comforter to every stuffed toy he'd been able to order straight from the biggest department store in Dallas. Even Cody had been bowled over by the assortment he'd assembled practically overnight. Melissa's mouth was agape as she surveyed the room.

"Did he buy out the store?" Melissa asked.

Before Cody could respond, Sharon Lynn was trying to scramble down, her gaze fixed on the rocking horse.

"Mi'ty, Mi'ty," she called joyously as she dropped from unsteady legs to her knees to crawl toward it. She pulled herself up beside it and tried to climb on. Cody lifted her up and settled her on the seat, keeping a firm grip on the waistband of her pants as she rocked enthusiastically.

He grinned at Melissa. "Told you she was going to be a natural on horseback."

"I think this one is a little more her size," Melissa retorted dryly. "The distance to the ground isn't quite so far."

Before he could comment on that, something else caught Sharon Lynn's eye and she twisted around and tried to clamber down. Cody lifted her off the rocking horse and set her back on her feet.

"How about you walk wherever you want to go this time?" he suggested.

Sharon Lynn clamped her fingers around his, wobbled precariously, then took an unsteady tiptoe step forward. With each step her confidence obviously mounted, though she kept that tight grip on his fingers.

"She's going to ruin your back," Melissa observed. "You're bent practically double."

Cody didn't give a hoot. This was the first time he'd witnessed his daughter's faltering, tentative footsteps. He'd bend over the rest of the afternoon and ache for a week, if she wanted to keep walking. With every minute he spent with her, every experience they shared, the powerful sense of connection he felt with her intensified.

Just then she stumbled and fell. Her eyes promptly filled with tears. Certain that she must have broken something to be sobbing so pathetically, Cody knelt beside her and gently examined ankles, arms, knees and elbows. He even checked for a bump under her hair or on her forehead, though he knew perfectly well she hadn't hit her head. She'd landed squarely on her well-padded button.

Finally satisfied that she was more scared than hurt, he scooped her up, only to find Melissa grinning at him.

"And you thought I was overreacting. At this rate, you're going to be a wreck in a month," she chided, sounding smug. "Either that or you'll drive the emergency room staff at the hospital completely wild. They'll flee when they spot you coming."

He lifted his eyebrows. "Is this another chunk of that learning curve you're trying to help me skip?" he taunted.

To his amusement, she blushed furiously. "Stop teasing. I only took her in twice," she admitted defensively.

"Oh? When?"

"The first time I thought she'd swallowed the toy from a box of cereal."

Cody shuddered. He would have had her in for X rays himself. "Had she?"

"No, I found it later in the crack between the refrigerator and the sink. I suppose she threw it across the room."

"And the other time?"

"She fell and bumped her head," Melissa said, shivering visibly at the recollection. "It terrified me. I'd never seen so much blood in my entire life. I was sure she was going to bleed to death before I got her to the hospital.''

Cody's heart skidded to a halt. He anxiously studied Sharon Lynn's face for some sign of such a traumatic injury. He smoothed back her hair to get a better look at her forehead.

''No stitches?'' he asked when he could find no evidence of them.

Melissa shrugged. ''Not a one,'' she confessed. ''They put a butterfly bandage on it and sent us home. Apparently head injuries just bleed profusely. There was no permanent damage done.''

Cody met her gaze and caught the faint signs of chagrin and laughter in her eyes. He also thought he detected something else, perhaps a hint of resentment that she'd been left to cope with such things on her own. Guilt sliced through him, even though part of the blame for his absence could be laid squarely at Melissa's feet.

''I'm sorry I wasn't here for you,'' he said, and meant it. He regretted every lost opportunity to share in the experiences—good or bad—of his daughter's first year.

The laughter in Melissa's eyes died at once. That hint of resentment burned brighter. ''I handled it,'' she said abruptly, and turned away.

He watched as she walked over and knelt down by their daughter, listening intently to Sharon Lynn's nonsensical jabbering. The hard expression on her face when she'd turned away from him softened perceptibly. A smile tugged at her lips as she cupped her hand possessively behind her daughter's head, caressing the soft curls. Sharon Lynn looked up at her, an expression of adoration on her face.

In that instant Cody saw what it meant to be a family... and he wasn't a part of it. Melissa couldn't have shut him out any more effectively, any more deliberately, if she'd tried.

He stood there, so close and yet very much apart from them. Longing welled up inside him, longing to know all of these little details of Sharon Lynn's first months that Melissa shared so grudgingly.

There was so much more he yearned for, as well. He yearned to share their closeness, to have Melissa look into his eyes with something more than distrust.

He sighed then, because it all seemed so unlikely, so impossible, thanks to his own foolish decision to accept what he'd seen that fateful night at face value. If only he'd stayed. If only...

Wasted regrets, he chided himself. This was his reality—a child who barely knew him, a woman who wanted no part of him, who was willing to allow him glimpses of his child out of a sense of obligation, not love.

He thought then of the flicker of passion he'd caught once or twice in Melissa's sea green eyes, of the heat that had flared when he'd touched her, and wondered whether her disdain ran as deep as she wanted him to believe.

Reality and circumstances could change, he reassured himself. Sometimes for the worse, of course. Harlan knew all about the dramatic, unexpected, tragic turns life could take. He'd lost a son and his beloved wife when he'd least expected it. Those losses had taught a lesson to all of them.

Harlan had also taught his sons that they could control most aspects of their lives if they set their minds to it and fought for what they wanted. In fact, he'd turned out a dynasty of control freaks, it seemed. Luke had built his own ranch from the ground up, rather than take the share in White Pines that Harlan had wanted him to have. Jordan had fought his father bitterly for a career in the oil industry. Cody had battled for a share of White Pines, and now, it seemed, he had an even more difficult war to wage.

Cody's gaze settled on Melissa and his daughter once again. They were worth fighting for. Harlan had given him years of practice at battling for everything from permission to go to a dance to the right to build his own house on White Pines' land. Apparently it had all been preparation for a moment like this.

His mouth curved into a slow smile. He'd just have to think of Melissa's rejection not as a setback but as a challenge. It was an opportunity to utilize all those lessons Harlan had not-so-subtly instilled in them. He would have to seize the initiative and keep Melissa thoroughly off kilter until she finally woke up and realized that this time he wasn't running.

This time he intended to be the steadying influence in her life and he meant to be there always.

Chapter Ten

The morning had been far too intense, Melissa thought as she finally escaped the house and settled gratefully into a chair on the patio with a tall glass of iced tea. The day had turned unseasonably warm and though she still needed her jacket, it was pleasant to sit outside in the fresh, clean air with the sun on her face while Sharon Lynn napped.

Her emotions were raw. Coming back to White Pines had been far more difficult than she'd anticipated. Part of that was because she felt Mary Adams's death here in a way it hadn't struck her even at the funeral. Some of it had to do with Harlan's warmhearted welcome and the obvious delight he was taking in getting to know his new granddaughter. Most of it, though, undeniably had to do with Cody.

At White Pines she was on his turf. Like Harlan, he reigned over the operation of this ranch as comfortably as she served burgers at Dolan's. His self-confidence radiated from him in this environment. It always had.

Cody might have been wickedly flirtatious and carefree in his social life, but when it had come to work he'd been mature and driven to prove himself to his father. His early success as a ranch manager had smoothed away any insecurities he might have had living in Harlan Adams's shadow.

Cody's command of this privileged world, combined with seeing how easily Sharon Lynn had been accepted into it as Cody's child, had caused her to rebel. Earlier, as Sharon Lynn had taken a few faltering steps with Cody's help, Melissa had had this awful, selfish feeling that Cody was benefiting from having a daughter without having done anything to deserve it beyond making her pregnant in the first place.

He hadn't coached her through labor. He hadn't walked the floor with Sharon Lynn in the middle of the night. He hadn't fretted and cried trying to figure out a way to calm her, all the while convinced he was a failure at parenting. He hadn't been there to panic over the sight of the blood from that cut she had described to him earlier.

No, he had simply waltzed back into their lives and expected to claim his parental rights by flashing his charming grin and dispensing toys like some cowboy Santa. Well, she wouldn't have it. She wouldn't let it be that easy. He was going to have to earn a right to be a part of his daughter's life . . . and of hers.

That decided, she was troubled only by the realization that her demands were vague, that even she might not recognize when Cody had paid the dues she expected. Should she have a checklist? A timetable? Or would she finally know somewhere deep inside when she was through punishing him for being absent when she'd needed him the most?

"You okay?" Harlan asked, coming out of the house and studying her worriedly.

"Fine," she said, fighting not to take her annoyance at Cody out on his father.

Harlan was innocent in all of this. She had seen for herself the toll his wife's death had taken on him and she was glad that bringing Sharon Lynn here had given him some pleasure. She was sorry that she had so stubbornly resisted the temptation to announce to all the world long ago that her child was Cody's, just so that Harlan and Mary might have had the chance to know their grandchild from day one. The irony, of course, was that everyone in town had known it anyway.

"If you're so fine, how come you're sitting out here in the cold all by yourself, looking as if you just lost your last friend in the world?" Harlan asked.

"I didn't lose him," she said dryly. "I'm thinking of killing him."

Harlan's blue eyes twinkled at her feisty tone. "Ah, I see. Cody can be a bit infuriating, I suppose."

"There's no supposing about it. He is the most exasperating, egotistical . . ."

"Talking about me?" the man in question inquired.

He spoke in a lazy drawl that sent goose bumps dancing down Melissa's spine despite her resolution to become totally immune to him. Obviously she still needed to work harder on her wayward hormones.

"Which part clued you in?" she inquired. "Exasperating or egotistical?"

Harlan chuckled at the exchange, then promptly clamped his mouth shut in response to a dire scowl from his son. "Sorry," he said insincerely. "You two want to be left alone, or should I stick around to referee?"

"Stay," Melissa encouraged just as Cody said, "Go."

"Thank you, Melissa," Harlan said, winking at her. "I think I'll stay. The show promises to be downright fascinating. This time of day, good entertainment's hard to come by. Nothing but cartoons on TV."

"Daddy!" Cody warned.

"Yes, son?"

"We don't need you here," Cody insisted rudely.

"Speak for yourself," Melissa shot back.

Cody strolled closer until he was standing practically knee-to-knee with her. He bent down, placed his hands on the arms of the chair and said very, very quietly, "Do you really want him to hear our private, personal, *intimate* conversation?"

The gleam in his eyes was pure dare. Melissa swallowed hard. Surely Cody was just taunting her. She couldn't imagine him saying anything to her that Harlan shouldn't hear. And the truth of it was, she wanted Harlan here as a buffer just to make sure that the conversation stayed on a relatively impersonal track. She didn't trust those slippery hormones of hers. They were liable to kick in when she least expected it.

She shot a defiant look at the man who was scant inches from her face. "Yes," she said emphatically.

Cody appeared startled by the firm response. His lips twitched with apparent amusement.

"Suit yourself, Me . . . liss . . . a."

The breath fanning across her cheek was hot and mint-scented. The glint of passion in his eyes sent her pulse skyrocketing. She tried to avoid that penetrating look, but no matter how she averted her gaze she seemed to lock in on hard, lean muscle. Temptation stole her breath.

She saw the precise instant when Cody's expression registered smug satisfaction, and it infuriated her. It galled her that she responded to him, annoyed her even more that he clearly knew it.

She gathered every last ounce of hurt and resentment she'd ever felt toward him to slowly steady her pulse. With careful deliberation she lifted her glass of tea to her lips and took a long, deep swallow. She kept her gaze riveted to his as she drank, determined to show him that this latest tactic no longer had the power to rattle her. He would not win her over with his easy charm.

Yet even as she did, even as uncertainty and then a flash of irritation darkened Cody's eyes, she quaked inside and prayed he would back off before she lost the will for the battle. She was weakening already, her palms damp, her blood flowing like warm honey.

Just when she was sure she could no longer maintain the calm, impervious facade, Cody jerked upright, raked a hand through his hair and backed off.

"Score one for Melissa," Harlan said softly, his voice laced with laughter.

Cody whirled on him. "Daddy, I'm warning you..."

Harlan's dark brows rose. "Oh?"

Cody frowned. "Dammit, how come you two are in cahoots?"

"Not me," his father protested, his expression all innocence except for the sparkle in his eyes that was quintessential Harlan. "I'm just a bystander."

"An unwanted bystander," Cody reminded him.

"Speak for yourself," Melissa retorted once again.

Cody scowled down at the two of them for another minute, then muttered a harsh oath under his breath and stalked off. Only when he was out of sight did Melissa finally allow herself to relax.

"Whew! That was a close one," Harlan said, grinning at her. "Another couple of seconds and the heat out here would have melted steel. Scorched me clear over here. You sure have figured out how to tie that boy in knots."

To her amazement, he sounded approving. "Shouldn't you be on his side?" Melissa inquired.

"I suspect Cody can take care of himself," he observed. "I'm just relieved to see that you can, too."

Melissa met his amused gaze and finally breathed a sigh of relief. She grinned at him. "It's about time, don't you think?"

"Way past time, I'd say," he said, and reached over to pat her hand. "You want some advice from a man who knows Cody just about as well as anyone on earth?"

"I suspect I could use it," she agreed, wondering at the turn of events that had truly put her and Harlan Adams in cahoots, just as Cody had accused. Maybe Harlan's wisdom would be more effective than his wife's advice had been.

"Despite all these centuries that have passed, the caveman instinct hasn't entirely been bred out of us men," Harlan began. "Now I know that's not so politically correct, but it's the truth of it. A man needs to struggle to claim what he wants. It builds up his passion for it, makes him stronger. Call it perversity, but things that come too easily don't mean so much. Don't ever tell 'em I said so, but I made every one of my sons fight me to earn the right to become his own man. They resented me at the time, but in the end they were better for it."

Sorrow flitted across his face as he added, "Except maybe for Erik. He wanted to please too badly. I made a serious miscalculation by forcing him to work in ranching, one I'll regret to my dying day."

Listening to his philosophy about men, Melissa wondered if Mary Adams had put up much of a struggle. Her adoration of Harlan, her catering to his every whim, had been obvious to anyone who knew the two of them. Given Mary's advice to her about making Cody jealous, Melissa suspected she had given her husband fits at one time.

"Did Mary make you jump through hoops?" she asked.

"She did, indeed," Harlan told her, chuckling even as his expression turned nostalgic. "I knew the first minute I laid eyes on her that she was the woman I wanted to marry. She was smart as the dickens, beautiful and willful. She claimed later that she fell in love at first sight, too. She didn't let me know it for a good six months, though. In fact, for a while there I was convinced she couldn't stand to be in my presence. It was a hell of a blow to my ego."

He shook his head. "My goodness, the things I used to do just to earn a smile. That smile of hers was worth it, though. It was like sunshine, radiating warmth on everyone it touched. For thirty-six years, I was blessed with it."

"You're missing her terribly, aren't you?" Melissa said softly.

"It's as if I lost a part of myself," Harlan admitted, then seemed taken aback that he'd revealed so much. He drew himself up, clearly uncomfortable with the out-of-character confidences. "Enough of that now. You didn't come all the way out here to listen to me go on and on."

"May I ask you a question?" Melissa asked impulsively.

"Of course you can. Ask me anything."

"Did you know Cody had asked me to marry him?"

"He told me."

"Did he also tell you I'd turned him down?"

Harlan nodded.

She looked over at this man who had always been so kind to her, who'd treated her as a daughter long before she had any ties to his family beyond her hope of a future with his son. Did she dare ask him what she really wanted to know, whether Cody loved her for herself or only as the mother of the daughter he was so clearly anxious to claim? She hedged her bets and asked a less direct question.

"Was I wrong to say no?"

Harlan regarded her perceptively. "Are you afraid he won't ask again?"

She drew in a deep breath, then finally nodded, acknowledging a truth that was far from comforting.

"What would you say if he does?"

"Right now?"

"Right now," he concurred.

She thought it over carefully. Given the unresolved nature of their feelings, she would have to give him the same answer. "I'd tell him no," she admitted.

"Then there's your answer," he reassured her. "Look, I don't claim to know what happened between you and Cody that made him run off to Wyoming, but it's plain as day to me that it wasn't a simple misunderstanding. You keeping that baby a secret from him proves that. Feelings that complicated take time to sort out. Take as long as you want, just don't shut him out of your life in the meantime. Silence and distance aren't the way to patch things up."

Harlan's warning was still echoing in her head when she finally went in search of Cody. He was right, the lines of communication did need to remain open, for Sharon Lynn's sake, if not her own.

She suspected Cody was either in the barn or had taken off for his own place nearby. His father had promised to look in on Sharon Lynn and to entertain her if she awakened from her nap.

When she didn't find Cody in the barn, she set off across a field to the small house Cody had built for himself in defiance of his father's order that he should strike out on his own and work some other ranch, maybe even start his own as Luke had. Every board Cody had hammered into place, every shingle he had laid on the roof had been a declaration that he intended to stay and claim his share of White Pines.

Melissa had watched him night after night, at the end of long, backbreaking days running the ranch. She had helped when she could, bringing him picnic baskets filled with his favorite foods on the evenings when he'd skipped supper to keep on working until the last hint of daylight faded.

She had observed his progress with her heart in her throat, waiting for him to ask her opinion on the size, the style, the color of paint, anything at all to suggest he intended it to be their home and not just his own. Though he had seemed to welcome her presence and her support, those words had never come.

Even so, she had been there with him when the last detail was completed, when the last brushstroke of paint had covered the walls. Though she had only spent a few incredible, unforgettable nights under that roof, she had always felt as if this was home. It was the place Sharon Lynn had been conceived.

As she neared the low, rambling white structure with its neat, bright blue trim, she thought she heard the once-familiar sound of hammering. She circled the house until she spotted Cody in the back, erecting what appeared to be a huge extension off what she knew to be the single bedroom.

The sight of that addition didn't snag her attention, however, quite the way that Cody did. He had stripped off his shirt, despite the chill in the air. His shoulders were bare and turning golden brown in the sun. A sheen of perspiration made his muscles glisten as they were strained and tested by his exertion.

Sweet heaven, she thought, swallowing hard. He was gorgeous, even more spectacularly developed than he had been the last time she'd seen him half-naked.

"Cody," she whispered, her voice suddenly thready with longing.

She heard the loud *thwack* of the hammer against wood and something softer, followed by an oath that would have blistered a sailor's ears. The ladder he was on tilted precariously, but he managed to right it and climb down without further mishap.

His gaze riveted on her, he muttered, "Damn, Melissa, don't you know better than to sneak up on a man when he's halfway up a ladder?"

She knew his testiness had more to do with his injured thumb than her unexpected presence. She grinned at him. "I've been in plain view for the last half mile. You would have seen me if you were the least bit observant."

"I'm concentrating on what I'm doing, not scanning the horizon for visitors."

"Just what is it you're doing?"

"Adding on."

She gave him a wry look. "That much is plain. *What* are you adding on?"

"A room for my daughter."

Surprise rippled through her. "Isn't that room Harlan's prepared good enough?"

"I want her to have her own room in my home," he insisted, giving her a belligerent look that dared her to argue.

"Seems like a lot of work for an occasional visit."

He climbed down from the ladder and leaned back against it, his boot heel hooked over the bottom rung behind him. His chin jutted up belligerently. It should have warned her what was coming, but it didn't.

"We're not talking an occasional visit, Melissa," he declared bluntly. "I expect to have her here a lot. You've had her for more than a year. I'm expecting equal time."

A year, here with Cody? Away from her? A sudden weakness washed through her. "You can't be serious," she whispered, thinking of the warning her mother had given her at the outset. Had Velma been right, after all? Would Cody bring all of the Adams influence to bear to get custody of his child?

"Dead serious," he confirmed, his unblinking gaze leveled on her.

This was a new and dangerous twist to Cody's driven nature. Clearly he intended to go after his daughter with the same singleminded determination he'd devoted to securing his place at White Pines.

"Cody, she's not a possession," she said in a tone that barely concealed her sudden desperation. "She's a little girl."

"A little girl who ought to get to know her daddy."

"I've told you—I've *promised* you—that we can work that out. I don't want to prevent you from spending time with her, from getting to know her, but to bring her to a strange house, to expect her to live with a virtual stranger...I won't allow it, Cody. I can't."

"You may not have a choice," he said coldly. "I don't want to get lawyers involved in this, but I will if I have to."

Melissa had no trouble imagining who would win in a court fight. As good a mother as she'd been, Cody and his family had the power to beat her. "There has to be another way," she said.

He nodded. "There is."

"What? I'll do anything."

His mouth curved into a mockery of a smile. "You make it sound so dire. The alternative isn't that awful. You just have to marry me."

The conversation she'd just had with Harlan echoed in her head. She couldn't marry Cody, not under these circumstances, especially not with him trying to blackmail her into it. What kind of a chance would their marriage have if she did? None. None at all.

She forced herself not to react with the anger or counterthreats that were on the tip of her tongue. Reason and humor would be more successful against the absurdity of what he was suggesting.

"Cody, half of the women in Texas would marry you in a heartbeat if you're anxious to have a wife," she said, refusing to consider the terrible consequences to her emotions if he took her up on what she was suggesting. "Why try to blackmail me into it?"

"Because you're the one who's the mother of my child," he said simply.

"But that's all I am to you," she replied, fighting tears. "It's not enough to make a marriage. At the first sign of trouble, what's to prevent you from bolting again, just like you did when you saw me with Brian? You don't trust me. You don't want me."

"Oh, I wouldn't say that," he said, straightening and walking slowly toward her with a look that flat-out contradicted her claim.

Melissa held her ground. If she backed down now, if she showed him any hint of weakness, he would win. The prize was more than her pride, more than her body. The prize they were warring over was her daughter.

Cody's advance was slow and deliberate. His eyes, dark as coal in the shadow of the house, seemed to sear her with their intensity. His lips formed a straight, tight line. Anger and frustration radiated from every masculine pore.

When he neared to within a few scant inches, the heat from his body enveloped her, tugging at her like a powerful magnet. And still she held her ground.

"I want you, Me...liss...a," he said quietly. "Make no doubt about that."

She shivered under his slow, leisurely, pointed inspection. Her skin sizzled under that hot gaze. The peaks of her breasts hardened. Moisture gathered between her thighs. Her entire body responded as if he'd stroked and caressed every inch of her. She ached to feel his fingers where his gaze had been. And still, unbelievably, she held her ground.

Her breath snagged, then raced. Her pulse skittered crazily. She longed for someplace to sit or lean, anything to keep her weak knees from giving away her shakiness.

"Tempted, Me...liss...a?"

"No," she squeaked, hating herself for not making the response firmer, more emphatic.

"Remember how it felt to have me inside you?" he taunted, hands jammed into his pockets, deliberately stretching faded denim over the unmistakable ridge of his arousal.

Her gaze locked on that evidence of his desire. A matching hunger rocketed through her. She swallowed hard, clenching her fists so tightly she was certain she must be drawing blood. But still she held her ground.

"In there, on that big, old, feather mattress," he reminded her silkily. "Our legs all tangled, our bodies slick with sweat. Remember, Me . . . liss...a?"

Oh, sweet heaven, she thought, desperately trying to replace his images with other, safer memories of her own. Memories of being alone and scared, when she realized she was pregnant. Memories of staring at a phone that never rang as day after day, then month after month ticked by. Thinking of that, she steadied herself and held her ground.

She leveled a look straight into eyes that blazed with passion and said, "It won't work, Cody. We can't resolve this in bed."

He reached out then, skimmed his knuckles lightly along her cheek and watched her shiver at the touch. "You sure about that, darlin'?"

She wasn't sure about anything anymore except the tide of desire she was battling with every last shred of her resistance. Her breathlessness kept her silent, afraid that anything she said or the whispered huskiness of her voice would give her away.

His fingers traced a delicate, erotic path along her neck, circling her nape, pulling her closer and closer still until their lips were a scant hairsbreadth apart, their breath mingling along with their scents; hers, wildflower fresh, his, raw and purely masculine.

The touch of his mouth against hers, gentle as a breeze, commanding as the pull of the tides, sealed her fate. The ground she'd held so staunchly gave way as she swayed into the temptation of that kiss.

Cody gave a sigh that she interpreted as part relief, part satisfaction. He coaxed her lips apart, touched his tongue to hers in a provocative duet.

Melissa bowed to the inevitable then. She had no power or will to resist this lure. She gave herself up to the sweet, wild sensations that had always been her downfall with Cody. He knew every inch of her, knew how to persuade and cajole, how to tempt and tease until her body was his as it had always been.

Her heart, she prayed, she could protect a little longer.

Chapter Eleven

The dare was backfiring. Cody knew it the instant he saw Melissa sprawled across his bed, her long auburn hair tangled on his pillow, her skin like smoothest satin, her coral-tipped breasts beckoning to him.

Until this moment it had only been distant memories that tormented him, fueling steamy dreams and restless nights. Now she was here and this throbbing hunger he felt for her was real. Powerful sensations he'd been telling himself that absence—and abstinence—had exaggerated were reawakened now with passionate urgency.

There might still have been a split second when he could have reclaimed sanity and reason, but if there was, he let it pass. His need for her was too great. His conviction that making love to her once again would bind her to him forever was too compelling.

The soft, winter sunlight spilled through a skylight above the bed and bathed Melissa in a golden glow. An artist might spend a lifetime searching for anything so beautiful, he thought as he stood looking down at her. An artist might spend an entire career trying to capture that same sensual vision on canvas and fail in the end. Cody certainly had never seen anything to equal the sight. He couldn't tear his gaze away.

Pregnancy had changed her body, gently rounding it, where before it had been all sharp angles and far more delicate curves. He swallowed hard as he absorbed the changes, regretting with every fiber of his being that he'd never seen her belly swollen with his child or her breasts when they were tender and engorged with milk.

He was aware of the instant when embarrassment tinted her skin a seashell pink from head to toe. She grabbed for a corner of the sheet, but before she could cover herself, he caught the edge and tugged it gently from her grasp. He stripped away his own clothes and sank down beside her, his gaze never leaving hers.

His breath eased out of him on a ragged sigh. "You are even more beautiful than I remembered," he said, touching his fingers to the pulse that hammered at the base of her neck, gauging her response. Her skin burned beneath his touch. Her pulse bucked like the most impatient bronco he'd ever ridden.

And her eyes, oh, how they pleaded with him. The delicate sea green shade had darkened with some inner turbulence. There wasn't a doubt in his mind that she wanted him with a desperation as fierce as his own.

He also knew with absolute certainty that she didn't want to desire him at all. Outside just now, she had fought her own passion valiantly, but nature and the inevitability of their mating were against her, just as they had been against him since his return to Texas.

He had always understood that internal war, perhaps even better than she did. Way back, when he'd waged his own battle to resist being hemmed in, when he'd struggled against commitment, his body had betrayed him, hungering for Melissa in a way he should have recognized as proof that they were meant to be. It had never been anywhere near as casual between them as he'd sworn to himself it was.

Now, with this second chance, his gaze intent, he skimmed his fingers over delicate skin, caressing new curves and exploring familiar planes. He scattered kisses in the wake of his touch, until her skin was on fire and her breath was coming in soft gasps and her eyes were the color of a stormy sea.

He wondered if he would ever understand the complex mix of raw, violent emotions she stirred in him. The primitive urge to claim and possess tangled with a more sensitive desire to awaken and give pleasure. He concentrated on the latter, judging the success of each stroke of his fingers, each dark and passionate kiss.

"Cody, please," she pleaded, her body arching upward, seeking his, seeking the very possession he held back.

"Not yet," he soothed, even as he intensified his touches, tormenting and teasing until he sensed that she was right on the edge of a shattering, consuming climax.

His own body was rigid with tension, his blood pounding hotly through his veins. He held his own satisfaction at bay with a will that was being tested beyond endurance. He had no idea if the torment was meant to incite Melissa or prove something to himself. Perhaps he was hoping for one last, tiny victory in his internal battle to demonstrate that she didn't have the power to captivate him so thoroughly, after all.

But of course, she did. And when her soft cries and his own demanding need could no longer be ignored, he slowly, *slowly* entered her, sinking into that moist, velvet sheath with a sigh of thrilled satisfaction. As the pace of his entry and retreat escalated, they rode each wave of pleasure together until willpower—his and hers—vanished in an explosion that made them one.

Afterward, still floating on the memories of that wild, incredible journey, Cody couldn't help thinking of the implication. Melissa was home at last, where she belonged . . . and so was he.

"I told you so," Cody murmured smugly sometime later, when the room was bathed in the last pink shimmer of a glorious sunset.

"Told me what?" Melissa asked, her eyes closed, her body tucked against his side.

"That being married to me wouldn't be so awful."

Her eyes blinked open and she rose up to lean on one elbow. "This isn't marriage, Cody," she reminded him with a scowl. "It's an interlude, one afternoon, nothing more."

He was stunned that she could be so cool, so dismissive, in the aftermath of such all-consuming heat and passion. "Are you saying that this meant nothing to you?"

"I'm saying it's not enough to make a marriage," she countered stubbornly. "Cody, if sex were all that mattered, you would never have left for Wyoming and we'd have been married long ago."

His temper snapped at that. "I would never have left for Wyoming if you hadn't deliberately tried to make me think you were becoming involved with my best friend," he shouted, flinging her responsibility for his leaving back in her face.

Even as he hurled the accusation, he climbed from the bed and yanked on his jeans. He stalked out of the bedroom, not sure where he was headed until he found himself outside on the deck, standing at the rail gazing over the land he loved. Not even such natural beauty had the power to soothe him now, though. Fury made his insides churn.

The quick escalation of the argument forced him to admit that Melissa was right about one thing: making love hadn't solved anything. If anything, it had complicated matters, because now they both knew that the explosive chemistry between them was as volatile as ever. It was going to be harder than ever to work things out with reason and logic, when the temptation was going to be to fall into bed.

He sensed Melissa's presence before he felt her slip up to the rail beside him. He glanced down and felt the sharp tug of desire flare to life all over again, proving the very point he'd just made to himself.

She had pulled on one of his shirts, which fell to midthigh, leaving her long, slender legs revealed. She'd cuffed the sleeves halfway up her arms. The sun turned her tousled hair to strands of fire. She looked part innocent waif, part sexy siren.

"It should never have happened," she said, meeting his gaze, her expression troubled.

"I don't—I *won't*—regret it." He studied her intently. "You do, though, don't you?"

"Only because it complicates everything," she said, echoing his own thoughts. "I want so badly to think clearly about all of this, to make the right choices this time. When you touch me, my brain goes on the blink. I'm all sensation and emotion and nostalgia."

"Stay here with me tonight," Cody blurted impulsively, suddenly wanting to seize the opportunity to force a resolution to their standoff. "Sharon Lynn will be fine with Daddy. Maritza will be there to help him look after her."

A wistful smile played around her mouth. "Haven't you heard a word I was saying?"

"All of them. I was just thinking, though, that we're both stubborn, strong people. Surely we could sit down and discuss all of this rationally and reach a sensible conclusion."

"Here?" she said doubtfully. "Within a few feet of that bed in there? Within a few feet of each other, for that matter?"

She was shaking her head before the last words were out of her mouth. "Forget it, Cody. It would never work. Besides, this isn't something we can resolve in a few hours or even a few days."

He sighed heavily. "So what do we do?"

"We give it time." Her expression turned rueful. "Preferably in very public places."

Cody wasn't wild about her solution. Now that he'd made up his mind to make the commitment he should have made two years earlier, Melissa's insistence on a delay was exasperating. He also feared that a decision reached on cold logic alone might not work in his favor. He wanted the heat of their passion on his side.

Of course, he reminded himself, their chemistry didn't necessarily confine itself to suitable locations. It could flare up just about anywhere, anytime, with the right look, the right caress. And there was something to be said for deliberately, provocatively stirring it up, when fulfillment was absolutely out of the question.

Yes, indeed, he decided with a renewed sense of anticipation, he could make things between himself and Melissa hotter than a day in the sweltering Texas sun. He could make it his business to drive her wild.

The plan had only one drawback that he could think of—it was very likely to drive him to distraction at the same time.

"Okay, you win," he said eventually, pleased when he noted the faint hint of disappointment in her eyes.

A less diplomatic man might have reminded her to be careful what she wished for. Getting her way obviously wasn't quite as satisfying as she'd expected.

"Let's get dressed and see what's happening up at the main house," he said, deliberately making it sound as if they'd just shared something no more personal than a handshake. "Sharon Lynn's probably awake by now. You shower first. I'll clean up the tools I left outside."

Melissa nodded at the bland suggestion and turned toward the house with unmistakable reluctance. Cody grinned at the dejected slope of her shoulders.

"Hey, Melissa," he called softly.

She glanced back at him over her shoulder, her expression uncertain.

"I'll be thinking about you in that shower," he taunted. "All wet and slippery and naked."

Color flared in her cheeks. The sparkle returned to her eyes. A pleased smile tugged at her lips as she turned and sashayed into the house with a deliberate sway of her hips.

Oh, my, yes, he thought as he watched her go. This was going to get downright fascinating.

If there was a decidedly knowing gleam in Harlan's eyes when they eventually returned to the main house, Melissa pretended to ignore it. What worried her more was that he might be getting ideas after their long absence that she and Cody had spent the time wisely and worked things out. Harlan believed strongly in family. He clearly wanted them to resolve things in a way that

kept them all together. Despite what he'd said earlier
about taking all the time she needed, hearing that they
had not settled a thing would surely disappoint him.

"I think we'd best be getting back into town," Melissa announced within minutes.

"What's your hurry?" Harlan asked at once.
"There's plenty of room here, if you want to stay the
night. I'm rattling around in this big old place all by
myself. It would be a pleasure to have company."

Melissa couldn't help thinking of another very re-
cent invitation to stay at White Pines, one she had
firmly declined. Her gaze caught Cody's and picked up
on the gleam of anticipation in his eyes as he awaited
her answer to his father's plea. She felt the web of Adams charm being woven snugly around her.

"No," she said, breaking free for now. "Another
time."

She scooped up her daughter. "Time to get home,
pumpkin."

Sharon Lynn promptly tried to squirm free, holding
her arms out plaintively toward her grandfather.
"Da?"

"You can come to see Granddaddy again very
soon," Melissa promised, forcing herself not to see the
equally wistful expression in Harlan's eyes as she refused to relinquish her daughter.

Harlan leaned down and kissed them both. "You're
welcome here anytime," he told her. "Both of you.
Don't stand on ceremony. Come whenever you have
some time."

"I'll walk you out," Cody offered, falling into step beside her. "Don't wait up for me, Daddy. I might spend some time in town tonight."

Melissa didn't have to glance back to know that the comment had stirred a speculative glint in Harlan's eyes.

"Why did you say that?" she demanded of Cody the instant they were out of earshot of the house.

He regarded her with his most innocent look, the one only a fool would trust. "Say what?"

"That you'd be staying in town for a while?"

"Because it's true."

"No, it's not," she said firmly. "We did not discuss anything about you coming into town."

"Who said I'd be with you?" he inquired, leveling a gaze straight into her eyes.

"But you said... W-who?" Melissa sputtered. "Dammit, Cody, you did that deliberately."

"Did what?"

"Let your father assume that you intended to spend the evening, maybe the whole night, with me."

"Is that what I said?"

"It's what you implied."

"You sure you're not projecting your own desires onto me?"

"No, I am not," she practically shouted, causing Sharon Lynn to begin to whimper. Melissa kissed her cheek. "Shh, baby. It's okay. Your daddy and I are just having a discussion."

Cody chuckled. "Is that what it is? You sure do get riled up over a little discussion."

"I am not riled up," she insisted, keeping a tight rein on her frayed temper.

"Could have fooled me."

"Oh, forget it," she snapped as she put Melissa into her car seat and buckled her in. As she walked around the car, she heard the driver's door open and assumed Cody was simply being polite. Instead she found that he'd climbed in behind the wheel.

"Now what?" she asked, regarding him suspiciously.

"I thought I'd hitch a ride."

"Why would you want to do that? It'll leave you stranded in town."

"Oh, I'm sure I can find someone willing to bring me home," he said, then winked. "Eventually."

He said it in a smug way that had her grinding her teeth. "Is that a new technique you've learned for luring ladies out to your place?" she inquired testily. "You claim to need a ride home?"

"Let's just say I'm trying it out tonight."

"And what if no one responds to your plight?"

"Oh, I don't think there's much chance of that," he said confidently. He shrugged. "If it does, I'm sure you'd be willing to take me in for the night."

"When pigs learn to fly," she retorted, irritated beyond belief that mere hours after they'd made love he was going on the prowl again. "Get out, Cody."

"I don't think so."

"Cody Adams, do not make me march back into that house so I can borrow a shotgun from Harlan."

He chuckled. "I'm not real worried about that, darlin'. You'd never shoot a man in plain view of his daughter."

He was right, of course. But, lordy, how she was tempted. "Oh, for heaven's sake," she muttered, flinging open the back door. "If you want to behave like a horse's behind, go right ahead."

"Thank you," he said, and turned the key in the ignition.

Cody was the kind of driver who liked to tempt fate. Melissa clung to the door handle, while Sharon Lynn squealed with excitement as they sped around curves. She knew they were perfectly safe. Cody never tried anything unless he was confident of his control of the road, the car, or the situation. In fact, she suspected that was exactly the point he was trying to make.

Even so, she was pale by the time he finally pulled to a stop in front of Rosa's Mexican Café. She was faintly puzzled by his choice. It was hardly a singles hangout.

"This is where you intend to spend your night on the town?"

He shrugged. "I thought we could grab a bite to eat first."

"Uh-huh," she said, regarding him skeptically.

"Do you have a problem with that?"

"Not really, I suppose, but you could have asked."

"I just did."

"Funny, it didn't sound much like a question to me. Maybe I already have plans for the night."

His expression turned dark. "Do you?" he demanded, his voice tight.

She let him wonder for the space of a heartbeat, then shrugged. "No, but I could have."

"Melissa, I swear..."

"Tsk-tsk," she warned, enjoying turning the tables on him, albeit briefly. "Not in front of the baby."

He scowled at her, scooped Sharon Lynn out of her car seat and headed inside, leaving Melissa to make up her own mind about whether to join them or remain in the car and quibble over semantics. Sighing over this latest test of her patience, she reluctantly followed him inside.

On a Saturday night, Rosa's was crowded with families. Melissa spotted Jordan and Kelly with their kids right off. Cody apparently did not, because he was making a beeline for an empty table on the opposite side of the restaurant. He picked up a booster seat en route and was already putting Sharon Lynn into it by the time Melissa joined him.

"Didn't you see Jordan and Kelly?" she asked. "They were trying to wave us over. There's room at their table."

"I saw them," Cody said tersely.

Melissa studied the set of his jaw. "Okay, what's wrong?"

"I do not intend to spend the evening with my brother," he said. "If you can call him that."

"Cody," she protested. "Why would you even say something like that?"

He frowned at her. "Because he knew about Sharon Lynn and he didn't tell me."

Melissa flinched as if he'd struck her. "Because I swore him to secrecy," she reminded him. She didn't want this family split on her conscience.

"He should have told me," Cody repeated, his stubbornness kicking in with a vengeance.

Melissa regarded him with a mix of frustration and dismay. The last thing she had ever wanted was to cause a rift between the two brothers. Uncertain what she could do to mend it, she turned and walked away. Cody was on her heels in a flash.

"Where are you going?" he asked suspiciously, latching onto her elbow.

"To the ladies' room," she said.

"Oh." He released her at once. "Sorry."

Melissa rolled her eyes and continued on to the back, praying that Kelly would spot her and join her.

She was combing her hair when Jordan's wife came into the rest room. "What are we going to do about them?" Melissa asked at once.

"It's not Jordan," Kelly said. "He feels terrible about what happened. He doesn't blame Cody for being furious."

"Okay, then, how do I get through to Cody? It's my fault. I've told him that, but he says Jordan should have ignored my wishes."

"He probably should have," Kelly concurred. "I could have told Cody myself and I didn't. There's enough blame to go around. The point now is to make things right. I wanted it settled before the baptism tomorrow so that Cody could be J.J.'s godfather. But until this is resolved, Jordan and I have decided to postpone the ceremony. It was only going to be a small family gathering anyway.''

''Maybe if Jordan made the first move,'' Melissa suggested.

Kelly shook her head. ''It wouldn't work. This is Cody's call, I'm afraid. The trouble is, we're dealing with the stubborn Adams men here.''

''Can you all stick around?'' Melissa asked. ''I'll think of something.''

''Sure,'' Kelly agreed. ''Our dinner's just now being served anyway. I can't imagine what you can do, but let me know if you think I can help.'' She paused on her way to the door. ''By the way, it's good to see the two of you together again. How are things going?''

''Don't ask,'' Melissa said.

Kelly grinned. ''That good, huh? Does that mean you haven't signed up at the Neiman-Marcus bridal registry yet?''

''No, and I wouldn't be holding my breath for that if I were you. I am not inclined to marry a man who is as thoroughly, unrepentantly, exasperating as Cody is.''

''Interesting,'' Kelly murmured, a knowing twinkle in her eyes.

''Don't start with me. I've just been subjected to Harlan's knowing looks for the past few hours.''

''Not another word,'' Kelly promised readily. ''Nobody understands the perverse streak that runs in this family any better than I do.''

After Kelly had gone, Melissa slowly put her comb into her purse and headed back to their table. She saw at once that Cody had been joined by Kelly's precocious six-year-old, Dani.

"I came to see the baby," Dani announced when Melissa had joined them. "She's cuter than my brother. I wanted a sister, but somebody got mixed up and gave me a brother instead."

Melissa grinned at her. "I bet you'll be glad of that when you're older. I always wished I had a brother who'd look out for me." She shot a pointed look at Cody when she said it.

Cody rolled his eyes. Clearly, he didn't think Jordan had done such a terrific job of looking out for him when it counted.

Dani stood closer to the table and leaned her elbows on it, propping her chin in her hands as she regarded her uncle. "You know, Uncle Cody, I was thinking."

He visibly contained a grin. "What were you thinking, you little con artist?"

"Maybe Sharon Lynn should have a kitten of her own."

"Maybe she should." He glanced at Melissa. "What do you think?"

"I think you two were plotting this," Melissa charged, trying not to chuckle at the guilty expressions. "Sharon Lynn does not need a kitten. More importantly, a kitten does not need Sharon Lynn. She'd probably scare it to death."

Dani's brow knit as she considered the argument. "She's probably right, Uncle Cody. Babies don't understand about kittens. Francie thinks that my brother is a pest."

"A valid point," Cody agreed. "Maybe after Sharon Lynn gets to know how to behave around those kittens you talked me into taking, she can have one of her own."

"Good idea," Dani said. "Francie will probably have more by then."

"Over my dead body," Jordan said, arriving to stand behind his stepdaughter. "Hello, Melissa." He looked straight at Cody, who avoided his gaze. "Cody."

After a visible internal struggle, Cody nodded curtly.

Jordan stood there, looking uncharacteristically indecisive for another minute before sighing and saying, "Come on, Dani. Your dinner's getting cold."

When the pair of them were gone, Melissa said, "You were rude to him, Cody. He made an overture and you didn't even say hello."

Cody closed his eyes. When he opened them, his stubborn resolve seemed to be firmly back in place. "I had nothing to say to him."

"Cody, I'm the one who betrayed you, not Jordan. I'm the one you thought had cheated on you. I'm the one who kept it a secret that I'd had your baby. You're speaking to me. You've forgiven me."

She studied him intently. "Or have you? Are you taking all the anger you don't dare express against me because of Sharon Lynn and projecting it on to Jordan?"

She saw by the way his jaw worked and his gaze evaded hers that she'd hit the nail on the head. She sighed. "Don't do this, Cody. Don't let what happened between us come between you and Jordan. Please," she pleaded.

When he didn't respond, she gave up. "Just promise you'll think about what I said, okay?"

"Yeah," he said tersely. "I'll think about it."

With great reluctance, Melissa finally conceded it was the best she could hope for. For now, anyway.

Chapter Twelve

Sometime well after midnight, Melissa woke to the sound of Sharon Lynn whimpering. She tumbled out of bed, flipped on the hall light and raced into the baby's room.

Sharon Lynn was tossing restlessly. Her skin was dry and burning up.

"Oh, baby," Melissa soothed as she scooped her up. "Are you feeling bad? Come with Mommy. I'll get you some water and check your temperature."

She had barely made it into the kitchen and flipped that light on when the front door burst open, scaring her half to death. She grabbed the frying pan and peeked through the kitchen doorway, prepared to do battle with a lunatic. Instead it was Cody, his clothes rumpled, his hair tousled, who stood in the foyer.

"Cody, what on earth?" she demanded, trying to slow the pounding of her heart. She set the frying pan down, though she wasn't entirely convinced he couldn't do with a good whop upside the head for scaring her so badly.

"What's going on?" he asked, casting worried looks from her to the baby and back. "I saw the lights come on. Are you okay?"

She ignored the question and tried to figure out what he was doing at her house in the middle of the night. The last time she'd seen him he'd been sitting at the bar in Rosa's. He'd declared his intention of starting his night on the town right there, clearly implying he intended it to end in someone's arms. She'd choked back her fury and tried to exit with some dignity, when all she'd really wanted to do was have a knock-down, drag-'em-out brawl with him. She was still itching for a fight, as a matter of fact, but right now Sharon Lynn's condition took precedence.

"Where have you been?" she asked, pleased that she was able to sound so cool when she was seething inside.

"On the porch," he admitted, taking his feverish daughter from her arms. As soon as he touched her, alarm flared in his eyes. "Good heavens, she's burning up. Have you taken her temperature?"

"I was just about to." She tried to remain calm in the face of his obvious panic and her own. She'd experienced rapidly spiking temperatures before and learned that it was a matter of course for children. Still, she'd never felt Sharon Lynn's skin quite so hot.

The thermometer registered one hundred and three degrees. Cody's face blanched when she told him.

"We're going to the hospital," he said at once, starting out of the kitchen.

Melissa blocked his way. "Not yet," she said far more calmly than she was feeling. There was no point in both of them panicking. "Let me give her a Tylenol and try bathing her with cool water to see if we can't bring that temperature down. If there's no change, then we'll call the doctor."

Sharon Lynn patted Cody's stubbled cheek weakly and murmured, "Da." She sounded pitiful.

Cody looked thoroughly shaken. "Melissa, I don't think we should wait. Something's really wrong with her."

"It's probably nothing more than the start of a cold or a touch of flu," she said. "Stuff like that reaches epidemic proportions this time of the year."

"Her temperature's over a hundred," he reminded her. "That can't be good for her."

"Babies get high temperatures. It's nothing to get crazy about," she insisted, amending to herself, *yet*.

She gave Sharon Lynn Tylenol, then ran cool water into the kitchen sink. "Bring her over here and let's get her out of that nightgown. It's soaking wet anyway. Why don't you go back to her room and bring me a clean one, along with a fresh diaper. We'll need those after I've sponged her off a bit with cool water."

Cody looked as if he might refuse to budge, but eventually he did as she'd asked. By the time he'd returned, Sharon Lynn was no longer whimpering. In fact she seemed to be relaxing and enjoying the cool water Melissa was gently splashing over her.

"Are you sure that's good for her?" Cody asked, worry etched on his face.

"It's exactly what the doctor and all the child-care books recommend. If you don't believe me, there's a book in the living room. Go read it." Anything to get him out of the kitchen again before he wore a hole in the linoleum with his pacing. Worse, she was feeling crowded with all of his hovering.

"No, no, I'll take your word for it," he said, standing over her shoulder and watching every move she made. "Maybe we should take her temperature again."

Melissa sighed and stepped aside to allow him to put the fancy new thermometer in Sharon Lynn's ear for a few seconds.

"It's a hundred and two," he proclaimed. "That's it. We're going to the hospital."

"It's down a whole degree," Melissa observed, blocking him when he would have snatched Sharon Lynn out of the bathwater. "The Tylenol's working."

"Not fast enough."

"Let's give it another half hour," she compromised.

Cody hesitated, then finally conceded grudgingly, "A half hour. Not a minute more."

He sat down at the kitchen table and fixed his gaze on the clock over the sink. Apparently he intended to watch each of those thirty minutes tick by.

"Da!" Sharon Lynn called out.

Cody was on his feet in an instant. "What's up, sweet pea? You feeling better?" he asked, caressing her cheek with fingers that shook visibly.

A smile spread across his daughter's face. "Da," she repeated enthusiastically.

A little color came back into Cody's ashen complexion. "She feels a little cooler."

Melissa agreed. "I'm betting when we check her temperature again, it'll be just about back to normal."

Twenty minutes later Sharon Lynn was no longer feverish. She was once again tucked into her crib. Cody, still looking shaken, stood over her.

"How do you stand this?" he murmured to Melissa. "I've never been so terrified in my life."

Melissa patted his hand. "It gets easier after you've been through it once or twice and know what to expect," she promised him, but he shook his head.

"I can't imagine it getting easier," he said. "What if her temperature hadn't gone down? What if you'd guessed wrong?"

"Then we would have called the doctor or gotten her to the hospital."

"It might have been too late."

"Cody, stop that," she ordered, not daring to admit that she'd been scared silly, too, that she always was, no matter what the books said. "It's over. She's going to be fine. It was just a little fever."

He closed his eyes and drew in a deep breath. "Okay, you're right. Just a little fever." He still sounded unconvinced. He definitely showed no inclination to budge from beside the crib.

Melissa grinned at him. "Cody, everything really is fine. You don't have to stand there and watch her all night."

"I am not leaving this house," he said, his jaw jutting out belligerently.

"Fine. You can sleep on the sofa." She yawned. "Good night, Cody."

"Where are you going?"

"Back to bed."

"How can you possibly sleep?"

"Because I'm exhausted. You must be, too." In fact, he looked as if he hadn't slept in days.

"I won't sleep a wink," he swore.

"Whatever," she murmured, and headed for her room. At the doorway she recalled that they'd never really talked about why he'd been on her front porch in the first place. "Cody, why were you here in the middle of the night?"

A sheepish expression spread across his face. "I figured if you found me on your doorstep in the morning, you'd give me a lift home."

She grinned. "Couldn't find another taker for that fabulous Adams charm, huh?"

"Never even tried." he admitted, then shrugged. "You've spoiled me for anyone else, Me ... liss ... a."

She studied his face intently, looking for signs that the comment was no more than a glib, charming lie. He appeared to be dead serious. A little flutter of excitement stirred deep inside her. Was it possible that Cody really did intend to stick around through thick and thin, through good times and bad?

For the first time since he'd come home from Wyoming, she dared to hope that he really had changed. If he had...

No, she cautioned herself at once. It was too soon to leap to any conclusions at all about the future.

"Good night, Cody," she whispered, her voice husky with a longing she would never have admitted.

"Good night, darlin'."

Cody felt as if he'd slept on an old washboard. Every muscle ached like the dickens. Every vertebra in his back had either been compressed, twisted or otherwise maimed by Melissa's sofa. He suspected she'd made him sleep there on purpose, knowing what it would do to him.

He also had the distinct impression that there was a tiny wanna-be drummer in his head flailing away without much sense of rhythm.

He groaned and opened his eyes, blinking at the sunlight streaming into the living room. That was when he realized that the loud clanging wasn't in his head. It was coming from Sharon Lynn's room. If that was the case, it just might be something he could stop before his head exploded.

Moving inch by careful inch, he eased to his feet and padded down the hall to the baby's room. When he opened the door a crack, he found her bouncing in her crib, banging a wooden block on the railing. The instant she spied him, a smile spread across her face.

"Da," she enthused, and held out her arms.

Cody wondered if he would ever get over the thrill that sweet, innocent gesture sent through him.

"Morning, pumpkin. I take it from all the commotion in here that you're feeling better."

"Ya ... ya ... ya."

"That must mean yes," he decided as he plucked her out of the crib and took the toy block from her as a precaution. His head was feeling marginally better, but another round of Sharon Lynn's musical skills would be a killer.

Her temperature seemed to be gone. He quickly changed her, then carried her into the kitchen. Once there, he was stymied. Was she old enough for regular cereal? Or was there some sort of baby food she was supposed to have? He didn't recall discussing breakfast when he and Melissa had shopped for groceries.

He settled Sharon Lynn into her high chair, found a soft toy bear to entertain her, and searched through the cabinets. Nothing conclusive there beyond an assortment of frosted cereals that seemed more likely to appeal to a one-year-old than her mother. Then again, he didn't know much about Melissa's breakfast habits, either. On the rare occasions when they'd slept in the same bed before he'd left for Wyoming, breakfast had been the last thing on their minds first thing in the morning.

A glance in the refrigerator suggested that juice might be a good place to start. He recalled buying an awful lot of apple juice at the store. He filled a bottle and handed it over. Sharon Lynn tossed her bear on the floor and accepted it eagerly.

Scrambled eggs struck him as a safe bet. Besides, he and Melissa could eat them, as well. Fixing one meal for all of them appealed to him. It struck him as cozy; a family tradition of sorts. Their very first.

He started the coffeemaker, popped four slices of bread into the toaster, put butter and jelly on the table, then broke half a dozen eggs into a bowl and whipped them with a fork until they were foamy. Suddenly he heard the faint sound of footsteps behind him. He pivoted around and discovered Melissa leaning against the doorjamb.

"My goodness, you've been busy," she murmured, yawning and bending over to pick up the bear Sharon Lynn had tossed aside in favor of her juice. "How long have you been awake?"

Goose bumps chased down his spine at the sleepy sound of her voice and the sight of that cute little fanny draped in a very short, very revealing, silk robe.

"Our daughter's better than any rooster I ever heard. She woke me at the crack of dawn."

"Obviously she's feeling better," Melissa said, going over to touch her hand to the baby's forehead. "No more temperature."

"Seemed that way to me, too."

"Did you take it?"

He shook his head, drawing a grin.

"Turning into an old hand already," she teased. "No more panicking."

"I wouldn't say that," he said, shuddering at the memory of that icy fear that had washed through him in the wee hours of the morning. "But I am going to borrow that book of yours and read it from cover to cover."

He reached for Melissa's hand and pulled her toward him. He was vaguely surprised that she didn't put up a struggle. Maybe he hadn't imagined the closeness between them the night before.

When she was standing toe-to-toe with him, he had to resist the temptation to tug the belt of her robe free. Instead he brushed a strand of hair back from her face and gazed into her tired eyes.

"You were wonderful last night," he said softly. "Not only were you good with Sharon Lynn, but you kept me from freaking out."

Her lips curved slightly. "Having you here helped me, too," she said, surprising him.

"Why?"

"Staying calm for your benefit kept me from freaking out myself," she admitted.

He stared at her in astonishment. "You were scared?"

"Terrified," she admitted. "But I knew I couldn't let you see it or you'd have insisted on borrowing your father's plane and flying us all to some critical care hospital in Dallas in the middle of the night."

"You've got that right." He grinned. "We're quite a pair, aren't we?"

"Just typical parents, Cody."

The simple words were no more than the truth, yet Cody felt as if he'd just heard something terribly profound spoken for the first time. He was a parent, a certified grown-up, with responsibilities he couldn't slough off. Responsibilities, in fact, that he actually yearned to accept.

He wanted more Sunday mornings just like this one, waking up to the sound of his daughter making some sort of commotion to get attention, fixing breakfast for all three of them, sitting at the kitchen table across from Melissa. He renewed his vow to himself to do everything within his power to convince Melissa they ought to be a family.

After they'd eaten and after he'd cleaned up most of the scrambled egg Sharon Lynn had managed to rub into her hair or fling halfway across the kitchen, he sat back with a sigh of pure contentment.

"Don't get too settled," Melissa warned, a teasing note in her voice. "Your daughter needs a bath. I think I'll let you do the honors since that egg she's smeared everywhere was your doing."

"You sound as if that's punishment," he said. "What's the big deal?"

"You'll see," Melissa retorted a little too cheerfully to suit him.

She ran the inch or so of bathwater into the tub, then left him to it. It didn't take long for Cody to figure out why she'd had that smug expression on her face when she'd exited the bathroom.

Sharon Lynn really loved water. She loved to splash it. She loved to scoop it up by the handful and dribble it all over him. She loved to throw her toys into it, sending yet more splashes into the air.

She wasn't quite so crazy about soap. She wriggled and squirmed, trying to get away from him. Slippery as an eel, she evaded capture until she'd managed to soak him from head to toe. In fact, he was fairly certain that he was wetter and soapier than she was.

Melissa chose that precise moment to reappear. He heard her chuckling as he tried to towel his daughter dry.

"You find this amusing?" he inquired softly.

"Mmm-hmm," she admitted. "I sure do."

He dipped his hand in the scant remaining water that was actually in the tub and splattered it straight in Melissa's smug face. A startled, incredulous expression spread across her face.

"You brat," she muttered, turning on the faucet in the sink and scooping up a handful of water to pour over his head.

Sharon Lynn squealed with glee as water splashed everywhere.

Cody nabbed a plastic cup from the counter behind him, dipped it into the bathwater and soaked Melissa's front. Only after the damp bathrobe clung to her body did he realize the mistake he'd made. His breath snagged in his throat at the sight of her nipples hardening beneath that suddenly transparent silk. He swallowed hard, aware of the tightening in his groin and the flood of color climbing into his cheeks—and equally aware of the impossibility of pursuing the desire rocketing through him.

Melissa's gaze locked with his for what seemed an eternity, then dropped to the unmistakable evidence of his arousal. A smile slowly tugged at the corners of her mouth.

"Serves you right," she taunted as she turned and padded off to her room.

Cody groaned and wished like crazy that he knew Melissa's neighbors so he could plead with them to baby-sit for the rest of the morning. He wanted to finish what she had started with that provocative taunt.

Instead he forced himself to concentrate on getting Sharon Lynn dried off and dressed. The task was somewhat complicated by the soaked condition of his own clothes. He was dripping everywhere.

As soon as he had his daughter settled in her playpen, he grabbed a towel, went into the laundry room, stripped, and tossed his clothes into the dryer. He wrapped the towel snugly around his waist and retreated to the kitchen to drink another cup of coffee while he waited for everything to dry.

When Melissa wandered in a few minutes later her mouth gaped. "Where are your clothes?" she demanded, her gaze riveted on his bare chest.

"In the drycr."

"Get them out."

"I can't wear damp clothes," he observed.

"Whose fault is it they're wet?"

"Yours, as a matter of fact," he said blithely. "You're the one who insisted I bathe Sharon Lynn. You obviously know what she's like in water."

She fought a grin and lost. "Yeah, I do," she admitted. "But, Cody, you cannot sit around in nothing but a towel."

"You have any better ideas?" He didn't wait for any suggestions from her before adding, "We could go back to bed."

"In your dreams."

He deliberately caught her gaze. "Absolutely," he said softly. "You have no idea how vivid my dreams have become lately."

From the fiery blush in her cheeks, he had the feeling, though, that he'd been wrong about that. He got the distinct impression that Melissa's dreams had been just as erotic as his own lately. He vowed that one day soon they'd compare notes...and make them come true.

Chapter Thirteen

The rapport between them lasted all the way back to White Pines. In fact, Cody had high hopes that he was finally beginning to make progress with Melissa. He was convinced that his presence during the previous night's medical crisis had started the difficult process of convincing her that he wasn't going to bolt out of their lives at the first sign of trouble.

It had been such a small thing, being by her side during those tense moments, but he'd heard the gratitude in her voice this morning, seen the first faint flicker of renewed faith in her eyes. He couldn't allow anything to shake that trust again, not until he'd had time to strengthen it.

As they drove up the long, winding lane at White Pines he was startled to see his father emerge from the house. It appeared Harlan had been watching for them and, from the too cheerful expression on his face and the contradictory worry in his eyes, Cody could only guess that there was bad news.

He stepped out of the car and faced his father warily. "Hey, Daddy, everything okay?"

"Fine, just fine," Harlan said too heartily. He darted a worried look at Melissa, then added, "You'll never guess who's here to see you, son."

Cody shot a desperate glance toward Melissa and saw that she was hanging on his father's every word. He couldn't imagine who might have turned up at White Pines uninvited, but experience with his father's demeanor suggested he was right to be concerned. He regretted more than he could say having Melissa here at this precise moment. He should have walked home, even if it was twenty miles. He would have if he'd had any idea that trouble was going to be waiting on the doorstep.

He drew in a deep breath and braced himself. "Who?" he asked just as the front door creaked open and a slight figure with cropped black hair and a pixie face emerged. Shock rendered him speechless.

"Janey? What the hell?" He looked to his father, but Harlan merely shrugged. Cody turned back to the teenager who'd apparently tracked him down and come after him all the way from Wyoming. "What are you doing here?"

Even as he sought answers for Janey's unexpected presence, he heard Melissa's sharp intake of breath behind him. Before he could turn around, the car door slammed with enough force to rock the sturdy vehicle on its tires. He knew what that meant. He forgot all about Janey as he tried to get to Melissa before she got the wrong impression and took off in a snit. Correction, she already had the wrong impression. He just had to stop her.

"Melissa," he protested just as the engine roared to life. "Dammit, we need to talk. Don't you dare drive away from here!"

He might as well have been talking to the wind. The order was wasted. She'd already thrown the car into gear, then backed up, spewing gravel in every direction. He slammed his fist on the fender as she turned the car, shifted again and headed away from the house at a pace that would have done an Indy 500 driver proud.

"Terrific," he muttered. "That's terrific. Not five seconds ago, I actually believed she was starting to trust me and now this!"

"Cody," his father warned, nodding toward the girl who had stopped halfway down the sidewalk.

Sure enough, Janey looked as if he'd slapped her. Cody raked his hand through his hair and tried to get a grip on his temper. It wasn't the teenager's fault that his personal life was a mess. He crossed to Janey Treethorn in three strides and looked into a face streaked with tears and eyes that were as wide as a doe's caught in the cross hairs of a hunter's gun. His anger dissipated in a heartbeat.

"Janey, don't cry," he said softly, pulling her into a hug. "Shh, baby, it's okay."

"I'm s-sorry," she stammered. "I didn't mean to mess up everything."

"I know," he soothed, awkwardly patting her back as he cast a helpless look at his father. Harlan shrugged, clearly as bemused by this turn of events as Cody was.

"It's not your fault," he told her, even though he very much wanted to blame her for ruining his fragile truce with Melissa. "Come on, let's go inside and you can tell me why you came all this way. Does your dad know you're here?"

"Ye-es-s," she said, sniffling. "Your father called him last night."

Cody's heart sank. Obviously, Janey had run away from home, if last night was the first Lance had heard of her whereabouts. His former boss was probably fit to be tied. Janey was the least rebellious of his daughters. If she had pulled a stunt as crazy as this, the other two were likely to drive him completely over the edge. Lance needed a mother for those girls and he needed her in a hurry.

Inside, Cody suggested that Harlan go and see if Maritza could rustle them up some hot chocolate. He knew it was Janey's favorite. There had been many cold winter nights when she'd fixed it for him and her father, then lingered in the shadows listening to them talk.

Before he sat down, he went into the closest bathroom and gathered up a handful of tissues and brought them back to her. He was careful to sit in a chair opposite her, since he had the terrible feeling that her crush on him was what had brought her all the way to Texas. He'd never done a thing to encourage it, except to be kind to her, but apparently that had been enough to cause this impulsive trip to Texas.

"Feeling better?" he asked after a while, when she appeared to have cried herself out and had finished the mug of hot chocolate Maritza had served with barely concealed curiosity.

Janey nodded, but wouldn't meet his gaze. Her cheeks were flushed with embarrassment. She tucked her jeans-clad legs up under her and huddled on the sofa like a small child expecting to be scolded. She looked so woebegone that Cody was having a difficult time maintaining what was left of his dying anger.

"Janey, tell me what this is all about."

"I c-can't," she whispered.

"There must be a reason you left Wyoming and came all the way to Texas. How did you know where to find me?"

"I found the address in Dad's papers."

"Did something happen at home?"

She shook her head, looking more and more miserable. Finally she lifted her chin and met his gaze for barely a second, then ducked it again. "You left," she said accusingly. "One day you just weren't there anymore and you never said goodbye."

Even though his reason for leaving had been an emergency, he could see how it might look from her perspective. He knew that in her reserved way, she counted on him.

"Didn't your dad tell you why I had to come home?" he asked.

"He said your mother died."

"That's right."

"But I thought you'd be coming back," she whispered. "But then you never did. And then Dad said you'd called and that y-you'd q-quit."

Her tears started all over again. Cody went for more tissues and brought back the whole box to buy himself the time he needed to figure out how to explain things to this shy, young girl who'd so badly needed someone that she'd chosen a miserable, cynical cowboy from Texas who already had a lousy track record for reliability.

"Janey, when I got here there were things that I realized I had to do. I couldn't come back. I explained all of that to your father."

"But...not...to me," she choked between sobs. "I thought you were my friend."

Cody sighed. "I am. I always want to be your friend."

"Then you'll come back as soon as things are settled here?" she inquired, hope written all over her tear-streaked face.

"No, sweetie, I can't come back."

"Why not?" she asked.

Not sure how she was likely to react, he drew in a deep breath before admitting, "Because I found out that I have a little girl and I have to be here for her."

Dismay darkened her eyes. "A baby?"

"Not so much a baby anymore," he confided. "She's over a year old."

"And you didn't know about her?"

"No."

Despite herself, she was apparently fascinated. For the first time since he'd arrived home, there was a sparkle in her dark eyes.

"How come?" she asked, her expression alive with curiosity.

"It's a long story."

"Was that her mom in the car just now?"

Cody nodded.

"Uh-oh," she murmured. Guilt and misery replaced the sparkle in her eyes. "I'm sorry if I messed things up for you, Cody. I really am."

He grinned ruefully. "Oh, the list of my sins is pretty long as it is. One more thing won't matter all that much."

"Want me to tell her you didn't know I was coming here?"

He had a feeling that the less Melissa saw of Janey, the better for all of them. Janey might be only fifteen, but she was a beautiful young girl who looked older than her years. It was the very fact that her body had blossomed so prematurely that had contributed to her shyness.

Ironically, he suspected she had been drawn to him for the very reason that he hadn't acted like the over-sexed teens who attended school with her. She'd felt safe with him, free to talk about her dreams, and she had magnified that feeling into a giant-size crush.

"No, sweetie, I'll take care of Melissa. Now, let's think about getting you back home again. How'd you get here?"

"I used my savings for a bus ticket. Then when I got to town, I called the ranch. Your dad came and got me."

Cody shuddered when he thought of her traveling that distance alone by bus. He also suspected that Harlan had deliberately not tried to track him down when Janey turned up to give him more time with Melissa before throwing a monkey wrench into things.

"I'll talk to Daddy about having his pilot fly you back to Wyoming," he told her.

Her eyes lit up. "Really?"

Her instantaneous excitement told him that her heart was already well on its way to healing. Maybe all she'd really needed was closure, a chance to say goodbye and make sure that she hadn't lost a friend. If he'd been half so insistent on closure before he'd taken off from Texas, maybe he and Melissa would have been married by now, instead of trying to rebuild their shattered trust.

Janey would be okay. He was sure of it. In the meantime, though, he had another heart to worry about. He had a feeling patching up the holes in Melissa's trust wasn't going to be nearly so easy to accomplish.

Melissa broke three glasses during the breakfast rush at Dolan's on Monday. As each one shattered, she heard a heavy sigh of resignation from Eli. She knew exactly how he felt. She'd had her fragile hopes shattered—again—the day before when she'd arrived at White Pines to find an adorable, sexy woman waiting on the doorstep for Cody.

As she swept up the debris from her latest round of clumsiness, she wished it were even half as easy to tidy up the aftermath of a broken heart.

When she finished sweeping, she glanced up and discovered Mabel sitting at the counter, curiosity written all over her face. To try to forestall the questions that were clearly on the older woman's mind, Melissa grabbed the coffeepot and poured her a cup.

"How about a Danish, Mabel?" she asked. "We have cheese and cherry left."

"No, thanks. So, did you and Cody have another fight?" Mabel inquired point-blank.

"No," Melissa replied honestly. They hadn't fought. She had taken off before her disillusionment could come pouring out in a wave of accusations.

"Now, why is it I don't believe that?" Mabel murmured. "You never broke a glass until that boy came back into town. Since then, you've been smashing them up so fast poor Eli's liable to go bankrupt."

"I'm going to reimburse Eli for the glasses," Melissa told her stiffly.

"No need for that," Eli called, proving that he'd heard every word of the discussion of her love life. "Maybe Mabel and I ought to sit that boy down and give him a stern talking to, though."

Mabel shot their boss a sour look. "What would you know about straightening out a lovers' tiff, old man?"

"As much as you do about starting one," Eli shot back.

Melissa stared at them. For the first time she noticed that their bickering carried the unmistakable sting of two former lovers. *Eli and Mabel,* she thought incredulously. Surely not. Then again, why not? She knew of no one else in either of their lives. Maybe that was so because they'd spent years carrying the torch for each other, unable to heal some foolish rift.

"Maybe I'm not the one who needs an intermediary," Melissa suggested, observing their reactions intently.

"You don't know what you're talking about," Mabel snapped. She shot a venomous look at the pharmacist. "Neither does he, for that matter."

"I know what I know," Eli countered. "Besides, we're not talking about you and me now. We're talking about Melissa and Cody."

"I'd rather talk about the two of you," Melissa said hurriedly, dying to know the whole story of two people who'd worked together as far back as she could recall without giving away so much as a hint that there was anything personal between them.

"No," Mabel and Eli chorused.

Melissa winced. "Okay, okay. We'll make a pact. You stay out of my personal life and I'll stay out of yours."

Mabel gave an obviously reluctant nod. Melissa waited for Eli to concur, but instead he muttered, "Too late. Yours just walked in the door."

Melissa's gaze shot to the front of the drugstore. Sure enough, Cody was striding in her direction, a glint of pure determination in his eyes.

"Go away," she said before he could settle himself on one of the stools.

"Is that any way to greet a paying customer?" he inquired.

He slapped a twenty on the counter. At the rate he was throwing them around, he was going to go broke.

"I'm not leaving until I've spent every last dime of that or you and I have talked," he announced. "You pick."

Melissa poured him a cup of coffee, snatched the twenty and tucked it in her pocket. "The coffee's on me. I'll consider the twenty a tip for services rendered."

Flags of angry color rose in Cody's cheeks. His grip on his coffee cup tightened, turning his knuckles white. "There's a name for taking money for that, darlin'."

Mabel sputtered and backed off her stool so fast it was still spinning a full minute after she'd gone. Melissa had a hunch she wasn't all that far, though, more than likely not even out of earshot.

"How dare you!" Melissa snapped.

"You started this round, not me," he said tightly. "Care to back up and start over?"

"We can't back up that many years," she retorted.

Cody visibly restrained his temper. Melissa watched as he drew in several calming breaths, even as his heated gaze remained locked on her. Her blood practically sizzled under that look. No matter how furious he made her, she still seemed to want him. It was damned provoking.

"Believe it or not, I came in here to apologize," he said eventually, his voice low.

"What's to apologize for? Just because you didn't mention that you were involved with another woman— a woman who apparently traveled quite some distance to be with you—that doesn't mean you owe me an apology."

To her annoyance, amusement sparkled in Cody's eyes. "I don't have a thing to hide, sweet pea. Want me to tell you about Janey?"

Melissa did not want to hear about the gorgeous creature with the exotic features, elfin haircut and sad, sad eyes. Cody had probably broken her heart, too.

"I can see that you do," Cody said, taking the decision out of her hands. "First of all, yes, Janey is from Wyoming. Second, I had no idea she was coming. Third, our relationship—then and now—most definitely is not what you think it was."

"Yeah, right," Melissa said sarcastically.

"Fourth," he went on as if she hadn't interrupted. "Her father was my boss, Lance Treethorn."

He leveled his gaze straight at her, until she felt color flooding into her cheeks. "Fifth, and most important, she is a fifteen-year-old kid."

Melissa stared at him. "Fifteen," she repeated in a choked voice. "Cody, that's—"

He cut her off before she could finish the ugly thought. "What that is, is a shy, lonely teenager with a crush on the first guy who didn't slobber all over her due to adolescent hormones," he insisted adamantly.

Melissa wanted to believe him. In fact, she did believe him. Cody was far too honorable a man to do anything so despicable. Harlan might have raised stubborn, willful, overly confident sons, but he'd instilled a set of values in them that was beyond reproach. She was the one who ought to be horsewhipped for even allowing such a thought to cross her mind.

She moaned and hid her face in her hands. "God, I'm sorry."

Cody shrugged. "Well, she does look older than she is. That's been her problem. The guys ahead of her in school think she's a lot more mature than she is and try to take advantage of her. She's coped by hiding out at the ranch."

"And you were kind to her, so she developed a crush on you," Melissa concluded, feeling like an idiot. "Why didn't you do something to put a stop to it?"

"For one thing, I had no idea it would go this far. The most overt thing she ever did before was leave food for me. She bakes a brownie that makes your mouth water."

Melissa grinned. "You always were a sucker for brownies."

"It was the first thing you learned to bake, remember? You were twelve, I think."

She remembered all right. Even back then she'd been trying to woo Cody by catering to his every whim. She wondered if it was ever possible to get beyond past history and truly have a new beginning. She'd been facetious when she'd snapped earlier that they couldn't go back far enough to start over, but maybe it was true. Maybe there was no way to ever get past all the mistakes and the distrust.

Despondency stole through her as she considered the possibility that they would never be able to move on.

"Melissa?" Cody said softly.

"What?"

"What's wrong?"

"Nothing."

"I don't believe that. You looked as if you were about ready to cry."

She tried to shrug off the observation. "Don't mind me. It's probably just Monday blues."

"I know how to cure that," he said. "Come out to White Pines tonight. We'll have a barbecue. It's warm enough today."

Melissa didn't think spending more time with Cody was such a good idea, not when parting suddenly seemed inevitable. Maybe Janey Treethorn's presence had been innocent enough, but sooner or later some other woman would catch his eye. They always did.

"The temperature's supposed to drop later," she said by way of declining his invitation. "It might even snow overnight."

Cody's expression remained undaunted. "Then I'll wear a jacket to tend the grill and we can eat inside."

"You never give up, do you?"

"Never," he agreed softly, his gaze locked with hers. "Not when it's something this important."

"What is it that's important, Cody?" she asked, unable to keep a hint of desperation out of her voice. "What?"

"You, me, Sharon Lynn," he said. "I want us to be a family, Melissa. I won't settle for anything less this time."

She heard the determination in his voice. More important, she heard the commitment. He sounded so sincere, so convinced that a family was what he wanted.

"Will you come?" he asked again. "You and Sharon Lynn?"

Melissa sighed. She'd never been able to resist Cody when he got that winsome note in his voice, when that thoroughly engaging smile reached all the way to his dark and dangerous eyes.

"What time?"

"Five-thirty?"

"We'll be there."

"My house," he said. "Not the main house."

Thoughts of making love in that house flooded through her. Melissa shook her head. "No," she insisted. "Let's have dinner with Harlan, too."

"Scared, Me . . . liss . . . a?"

"You bet, cowboy. You should be, too." She lowered her voice. "The last time we were alone in that house, we made love and we didn't take precautions. I'm not risking that again."

Cody grinned. "Hey, darlin', that's something I can take care of right here and now," he offered. "I'm sure Eli can fix me right up."

Melissa's cheeks flamed at the prospect of having Eli and Mabel know any more of her business than they already did. "Cody, don't you dare. Besides, we decided that sleeping together only complicated things."

"Did we decide that?"

"You know we did. We have dinner at Harlan's or you can forget it."

"Okay, darlin', I'll let you win this round," he said, startling her with his lack of fussing. "See you at five-thirty."

It wasn't until she arrived at White Pines that she discovered the reason for Cody's calm acceptance of her edict.

"Where's Harlan?" she inquired suspiciously the minute she stepped into the too silent foyer of the main house.

Cody's expression was pure innocence as he gazed back at her. "Oh, didn't I mention it? Daddy's gone to spend a few days with Luke and Jessie."

With Sharon Lynn already happily ensconced in her father's arms, with a huge stack of ribs just waiting to be barbecued, Melissa bit back the urge to turn right around and flee. This round, it appeared, had gone to Cody.

Chapter Fourteen

For the next two months, Cody won more rounds than he lost, much to Melissa's chagrin. Though she'd turned down his proposals every time he made them, he took the rejections in stride. He just redoubled his efforts to change her mind. Her resistance was in tatters. Her senses were spinning just at the sight of him. She was clinging to the last shreds of pride and determination she had left.

There were moments, she was forced to admit, when she couldn't even remember why she was so staunch in her conviction that marrying Cody was positively the wrong thing to do. He had done absolutely nothing since his return to indicate that he wasn't thoroughly absorbed in his relationship with her and their child.

He was sweetly attentive to her. He doted on Sharon Lynn.

And still, for reasons she was finding harder and harder to fathom, she kept waiting for some other woman to come between them, for some blowup that would send Cody racing away from Texas, away from them. It didn't seem to matter that his roots at White Pines ran deeper than ever. He'd left his home and her once before. She never forgot that, wouldn't let herself forget it.

She put more obstacles in their path to happiness than championship hurdlers had ever had to jump. Cody, just as determinedly, overcame each and every one, without criticism, without comment. He just did whatever was asked of him.

The truth of it was that his thoughtfulness and consideration were beginning to wear on her. She figured it was an indication of the depths of her perversity that she longed for a good, old, rip-roaring fight.

She was already working herself into a confrontational state when she reached her mother's after a particularly exhausting day at work, only to find that Sharon Lynn wasn't there.

"What do you mean, she's not here?" she demanded, staring at her father. Her mother was nowhere in sight, which should have been her first clue that her life was about to turn topsy-turvy.

"Cody came by," her father admitted. "I let him take her."

"You what?" Her voice climbed several octaves. Was everyone in town on Cody's side these days? She'd thought for sure at least her parents would stick up for her. Instead her father had joined the enemy camp.

"Why would you do that?" she asked plaintively.

Her father regarded her with amusement. "He's the child's father, for starters. He wanted to spend some time with her. He said he'd drop her off at your house and save you the trip. I guess he didn't tell you that, though."

"No, he did not," she snapped. "Which is a pretty good indication of why Cody Adams is not to be trusted."

"If you ask me, he's been jumping through hoops to prove he can be trusted. Why don't you give the guy a break?" He patted her check. "Come on, ladybug. You know you want to."

"I can't," she said simply.

"Why not?"

"Because he'll leave again at the first sign of trouble."

"He left before, because you provoked him into it. I can't say I blame him for being furious about finding you out with Brian. Going out with him was a danged fool idea to begin with."

Melissa's anger wilted. "I agree, but Cody should have stayed and talked to me. He shouldn't have run."

"Don't you think he knows that now?" her father inquired reasonably. "Don't you think if he had it to do all over again, he would make a different choice?"

"I suppose," she conceded reluctantly. "He says he would anyway."

"And aren't you the one who made things worse by refusing to tell him about the baby?"

She scowled at her father, the man who had stood by her even though he disagreed with her decision to keep Cody in the dark. "What's your point?"

"He forgave you, didn't he? Isn't it about time you did the same for him?"

Melissa was startled by the depth of her father's support for Cody. "How come you've never said any of this before?" she asked.

Her father's expression turned rueful. "Because your mother seemed to be saying more than enough without me jumping in and confusing you even more. Watching you getting more miserable day by day, I finally decided when Cody showed up today that enough was enough. I told her to butt out."

Melissa couldn't help grinning. "So there'd be room for you to butt in?"

"Something like that. Go on, cupcake. Meet Cody halfway, at least. For whatever it's worth, I think he's a fine man."

Melissa sighed. "So do I."

She made up her mind on the walk to her own house that she would try to overcome the last of her doubts and take the kind of risk her father was urging. There was a time when she would have risked anything at all to be with Cody. The pain of losing him once had made her far too cautious. It was probably long past time to rediscover the old Melissa and take the dare he'd been issuing for months now.

She found him in a rocker on her front porch, a tuckered out Sharon Lynn asleep in his lap.

"Rough afternoon?" she queried, keeping her tone light and displaying none of the annoyance she'd felt when she'd discovered he'd absconded with her daughter. She sank into the rocker next to him and put it into a slow, soothing motion. She allowed her eyes to drift closed, then snapped them open before she fell completely, embarrassingly, asleep.

"Playing in the park is tough work," he said, grinning at her. "There are swings and seesaws to ride, to say nothing of squirrels to be chased." His gaze intensified. "You look frazzled. Bad day?"

"Bad day, bad week, bad everything," she admitted, giving in to the exhaustion and turmoil she'd been fighting.

"I know just how to fix that," Cody said, standing. He shifted Sharon Lynn into one arm and held out a hand. "Give me the key."

Melissa plucked it from her purse and handed it over without argument. As soon as he'd gone, she closed her eyes again. The soothing motion of the rocker lulled her so that she was only vaguely aware of the screen door squeaking open and the sound of Cody's boots as he crossed the porch.

"Wake up, sleepyhead," he urged. "Here, take this."

She forced her eyes open and saw the tall glass he was holding out. "Lemonade?" she asked with amazement. "Where'd you get it?"

"I made it."

Her eyes blinked wider. "From scratch?"

He grinned. "I didn't bake a chocolate soufflé, sweet pea. It's just lemonade."

They sat side by side, silently rocking, for what seemed an eternity after that. The spring breeze brought the fragrance of flowers wafting by. Hummingbirds hovered around the feeder at the end of the porch.

"This is nice, isn't it?" Cody said eventually.

"Not too tame for you?" Melissa asked.

"Don't start with me," he chided, but without much ferocity behind the words.

She thought of what her father had said and of her own resolution to start taking risks. "I'm sorry. I didn't mean to say that. I guess it's become automatic."

"Think you can break the cycle?" he inquired lightly.

Melissa met his gaze. "I'm going to try," she promised. "I do want what you want, Cody."

"But you're scared," he guessed. At her nod he added, "Can't say that I blame you. I spent a lot of years hiding from the responsibilities of a relationship. Once you make a commitment, there's a lot riding on getting it right. I never did much like the idea of failing."

"Can I ask you something?"

"Anything, you know that."

"What makes you so certain we can get it right now?"

He grinned at the question. "You know any two more stubborn people on the face of the earth?"

Her lips twitched at that. "No, can't say that I do."

"I pretty much figure if we finally make that commitment, neither one of us will bail out without giving it everything we've got." He slanted a look over at her that sent heat curling through her body. "Nobody can do more than that, sweet pea. Nobody."

He stood, then bent down to kiss her gently. "Think about it, darlin'."

"You're leaving?" she asked, unable to stop the disappointment that flooded through her.

"If I stay here another minute with you looking at me like that, I'm going to resort to seducing you into giving me the answer I want. I think it'll be better if I take my chances on letting you work this one out in your head."

He was striding off to his pickup before she could mount an argument. She actually stood to go after him, but a wave of dizziness washed over her that had her clutching at a post to keep from falling.

What on earth? she wondered as she steadied herself. Suddenly she recalled the occasional bouts of nausea she'd been feeling that she'd chalked off to waiting too long to grab breakfast in the mornings. She thought about the bone-deep weariness that had had her half-asleep in that rocker only a short time before. And now, dizziness.

Oh, dear heaven, she thought, sinking back into the rocker before she fainted. Unless she was very much mistaken, every one of those signs added up to being pregnant—again.

* * *

How could this have happened to them a second time? Melissa wondered as she left the doctor's office in a daze the following morning. How could she be pregnant from that one time they'd made love at Cody's? They'd been so darned careful not to repeat the same mistake. She'd held him at arm's length, refusing to make love again for that very reason, because neither one of them used a lick of common sense once they hopped into bed together. It was better not to let their hormones get out of hand in the first place.

She had no idea what was going to happen next, but she did know that this time she would tell Cody right away. There would be no more secrets to blow up in her face later.

Dammit, why couldn't everything have been more resolved between them? They were so close to working things out. She had sensed that last night in their companionable silence, in the way Cody had vowed to give her the time and space to reach her own conclusions about their relationship.

She knew exactly how Cody was going to react. Forget about time and space for thinking. He was going to demand they get married at once. She wanted that, wanted it more than anything, but not if he was only doing it because of the baby. Okay, both babies.

He was a fine father. He'd accepted his responsibility for Sharon Lynn wholeheartedly. That wasn't the issue. He'd been proving that over and over since the day he'd learned the truth about Sharon Lynn. She had seen the adoration in his eyes whenever he was with his daughter. She had watched his pride over every tiny accomplishment.

He had even behaved as though she were important to him, too. But never once, not in all these months, had he said he loved her. She would not marry a man who could not say those words. She would not marry at all just because she was pregnant.

It created an interesting dilemma, since there wasn't a darn thing she could do about being pregnant. There was nothing on earth that meant more to her than being a mother to Cody's children. And she knew from bitter experience that she could do it just fine on her own, if she had to.

Still, she had to tell him sometime....

She managed to hold off for a couple of weeks, but her symptoms were cropping up when she least expected it. She didn't want him guessing when he found her practically swooning in his arms.

After thinking it over, she chose the storeroom at Dolan's to tell him. Eli and Mabel were getting used to her dragging Cody into the back to talk. They'd probably heard enough muffled arguments and full-scale screaming matches to last them a lifetime.

At least, though, they would be there to intervene if Cody decided to try to drag her off by the hair to the preacher. At home she'd have no such protection. She doubted even her parents would stand up to him. Her father was already on Cody's side and her mother had maintained a stoic silence ever since her father's edict that she butt out of Melissa's and Cody's business.

She had one other reason for choosing the storeroom. She had noticed that Eli and Mabel were off by themselves whispering who-knew-what at the oddest times. Melissa had the feeling that the two of them were patching whatever differences had separated them years before. Maybe the very visible ups and downs of her relationship with Cody had set an example for them. They might as well be in on the denouement.

When Cody walked through the door as he'd gotten into the habit of doing around closing every day, Melissa's hands trembled. This time nothing on earth could have persuaded her to so much as touch a glass in Cody's presence.

Not even giving Cody time to get settled, she drew in a deep breath. "We need to talk."

"Okay," he said, giving her that crooked smile that made her heart flip over. "What's up?"

"In the back," she said.

Cody groaned. "Not again."

She glanced at Eli and Mabel, who were both suddenly extremely busy, their backs to the counter. "Will you just come on?" she muttered, holding the door open.

Cody trailed along behind her and propped a booted foot onto an unopened shipment of new glasses. "What now?"

Melissa tried to gather her courage. Finally she blurted, "I'm pregnant."

Cody's eyes widened incredulously. "You're going to have a baby?"

She nodded, watching him carefully, not quite able to get a fix on his reaction.

"A baby?" Cody repeated.

"Yes."

"Oh, my God." He sank down on the box, which gave way just enough to shatter the two dozen glasses inside.

At the sound of all that cracking glassware, Melissa started to chuckle. Cody bounced to his feet, but there was no hope for the crushed shipment.

"You okay?" she inquired between giggles. "No glass in your backside?"

"Forget my backside. It's just fine. Tell me more about the baby. When is it due?"

"You should be able to figure that one out. We only slept together that once since you got back."

"I can't even add two and two right now. Just tell me."

"A little over six months."

He nodded. "Good. That's plenty of time."

Melissa regarded him suspiciously. "Plenty of time for what?" she asked, although she thought she had a pretty good idea of the answer.

"To get married," he said at once. "Finish fixing up my house at White Pines, decorate a new nursery."

Melissa held up her hands. "Whoa, cowboy. Who says we're getting married?"

A mutinous expression settled over his face. "I do. No baby of mine is going to be born without my name. It's bad enough that we haven't taken care of getting

Sharon Lynn's name legally changed. I'm not doubling the problem."

"Okay, say I agree to get married—which I haven't," she added in a rush when she saw the instant gleam in his eyes. "Then what?"

He stared at her blankly. "What?"

"Are you planning for us to live happily ever after? Are you intending to get a divorce as soon as the ink's dry on the birth certificate? What?" *Please,* she thought to herself, *let him say he loves me. Please.*

"You know better than that," he said.

It was a wishy-washy answer if ever Melissa had heard one. "Do I?" she shot back. "How? Just because you've been here a few months now and haven't taken off?"

He raked his fingers through his hair. "Yes."

"Not good enough, cowboy," she said, exiting the storeroom and emphatically closing the door behind her.

Mabel and Eli were suspiciously close to the door, though their attention seemed to be thoroughly engaged in their work. Of course, Mabel was sweeping the exact same spot she'd swept not fifteen minutes earlier and Eli was dusting off a shelf, a task that usually fell to Mabel.

"I'm leaving," she announced, grabbing her purse and heading for the door.

Mabel trailed her outside. "Don't be a fool, girl. Marry that man and put him out of his misery."

"I can't," Melissa said, sounding pretty miserable herself.

"Why the devil not?"

"He's only thinking about the babies. He's not thinking about us at all."

"If that's all he cared about, he could file for joint custody, pick them up on Friday afternoons and send you a support check," Mabel countered. "I don't hear him talking about doing any of that. He's talking about marriage, has been ever since he got back into town."

"Because it's the right thing to do," Melissa insisted stubbornly. "The Adams men are nothing if not honorable."

Mabel shot her a look of pure disgust. "Maybe you ought to be thinking about doing the right thing, too, if that's the case. Those babies deserve a chance at a real home. Cody's willing to give them that. Why can't you?"

Mabel's words lingered in her head as she walked over to pick up Sharon Lynn. They echoed there again and again as she fought every single attempt Cody made to persuade her to change her mind.

She told herself she wasn't the one making things difficult. All it would take to make her change her mind was three little words—I love you. They were about the only words in the whole English language that Cody never, ever tried.

Chapter Fifteen

From the instant he discovered that Melissa was pregnant again, Cody tried to persuade her to marry him. He coaxed. He wooed. He pitched a royal fit on occasion and threatened to hog-tie her and carry her off to the justice of the peace.

For six solid months he did everything but stand on his damned head, but Melissa seemed to have clothed her heart in an impenetrable sheet of armor. He surely didn't remember the woman being this stubborn. The whole town was watching the two of them as if they were better than any soap opera on TV. He found it mortifying to be chasing after a woman who acted as if he didn't even exist.

He also discovered that this new side of Melissa was every bit as intriguing as it was vexing. He realized that he'd always taken for granted that sooner or later she would admit she loved him and accept his oft-repeated proposal. That she was still turning him down with another baby on the way shook him as nothing else in his life ever had. Maybe this was one time when his charm wasn't going to be enough.

And the truth of it was, she seemed to be getting along just fine. He'd seen that for himself ever since he'd gotten back from Wyoming. She had made a nice life for herself and Sharon Lynn. She would fit a new baby into that life without batting an eye.

She was strong and self-sufficient, downright competent as a single parent. She had her job at the drugstore. She had friends who were there for her. She had parents who supported her in whatever decisions she made, though he sensed that her father was not quite as thrilled with this independent streak as her mother was.

In short, Melissa had a life, while Cody was lonelier than he'd ever imagined possible even in the dead of a rough Wyoming winter.

The thought of Melissa going into that delivery room with anyone other than him as her labor coach grated. The prospect of his baby—a second baby, in fact—being born without his name made him see red. He wanted to be a part of that baby's life so badly it stunned him.

What flat-out rocked him back on his heels, though, was the fact that he wanted to be with Melissa just as badly. Maybe he'd started out just saying the words, asking her to marry him because of Sharon Lynn and more recently this new, unborn baby. But sometime, when he hadn't been paying attention, he'd gone and fallen in love with the woman. Mature, adult love this time, not adolescent hormones and fantasy.

How the hell was he going to get her to believe that, though? Nothing he had done in the past eight and a half months since he'd come home to Texas had done a bit of good.

He'd been steady. He'd been reliable. He'd even managed to seduce her, which was what had gotten them into this latest fix. Melissa, however, had kept a stubborn grip on her emotions. She had refused to concede feeling so much as affection for him, much less love.

Cody was at his wit's end. He'd decided, though, that it was tonight or never. He was going to make one last, impressive, irresistible attempt to convince Melissa to be his wife. If it failed, he would just have to resign himself to this shadow role in the life of his children. Up until now he'd turned his back on his pride, but it was kicking up a storm for him to stop behaving like a besotted fool and give up.

He took hat quite literally in hand and went to visit Velma. He needed her help if his plan was to work. Responding to his knock on her door in midafternoon, she regarded him with her usual suspicion.

"What do you want?" she inquired ungraciously.

Cody lost patience. "I am not the bad guy here," he informed her as he stalked past her and stood in the middle of the foyer.

He could hear Sharon Lynn chattering away in the guest room. It sounded as if she were having a tea party. He longed to go down that corridor and spend some time with her. She was changing in one way or another every day and he hated to miss a single one. Today, though, he was on a mission here and he couldn't afford to be distracted.

"I came by to see if you could keep Sharon Lynn here tonight," he said.

"Why?" Velma asked bluntly.

"So that Melissa and I can have an evening together alone."

"Seems to me you two have found enough time to be alone without my help in the past. She's about to have a baby again, isn't she? She didn't get that way in public, I suspect."

Her sarcasm grated. Cody held back the sharp retort that came to mind. If this was going to work out, it was way past time he made peace with Melissa's mother. "Exactly what has she told you about our relationship?"

Velma didn't give an inch. "She doesn't have to say a word. I can see plenty for myself."

"What do you think you see, then?"

"That you think your money and your power give you the right to be irresponsible. You've used my daughter, left her, then come back here and used her again without ever giving a thought to the consequences."

"Are you aware that I have been trying to persuade your mule-headed daughter to marry me since the very first instant I got back into town?"

Velma blinked, but she didn't back down. Talk about stubborn pride. Velma had it in spades, which probably explained Melissa's streak of it.

"Too little, too late, if you ask me," she retorted.

Cody started to tell her he hadn't asked her, but of course he had. "Look, I don't blame you for resenting me, but the fact of the matter is that I love your daughter, stubborn as she is, and I want to marry her and be a father to our children. I think she loves me, too, but she thinks she's a fool for doing it."

He saw from the set expression on her face that Velma had probably reinforced that belief. Maybe if he could win over the mother, she'd change her tune with Melissa and give him a fighting chance.

"You want her to be happy, don't you?"

"Of course I do," she said indignantly. "What makes you think I don't?"

"Because I think she's taking her cue from you. I think if she and I had just a little time alone, we could work this out, preferably before another one of our children is born without my name. Will you give us that chance?"

Velma spent the next minute or two in an obvious struggle with her conscience. "What is it you want, exactly?"

"Keep Sharon Lynn here tonight. Don't interfere with my plans. That's all."

"You think you can convince her in one night, when you haven't made any progress at all in the past nine months?" Velma inquired with a shake of her head. "You don't know Melissa half as well as you think you do."

She sighed heavily. "Okay, I'll keep Sharon Lynn for you," she relented to Cody's relief. "But it'll have to be for the whole weekend. If you ask me, it's going to take you that long, maybe even longer, to turn that girl around. She's scared spitless she'll admit she loves you and you'll turn around and leave again."

"I won't," he swore. He circled Velma's waist and spun her around. "Thank you. You're an angel."

She kept her lips in a tight line, resisting him to the bitter end, but Cody thought he detected a spark of amusement in her eyes. "See that you do right by her, young man, or I'll have your hide."

He kissed her cheek. "Not to worry, Velma. This is going to be a weekend to remember."

He was already making plans to sweep Melissa away to a quiet, secluded cabin for a romantic weekend by the time he hit the driveway.

His first stop was her house, where he managed to sneak in without being caught by the sheriff or a neighbor. He rummaged through her drawers and closets to find lingerie and the prettiest, sexiest maternity clothes she owned. He packed them, along with perfume and cosmetics, praying that he got the right ones. He didn't want her dissolving into tears because he couldn't find her blush or her mascara. Her hormones had her reacting in the most bizarre ways these days. He figured he ought to get a whole lot of points for just managing to stick by her anyway.

He'd considered taking her off to someplace fancy, maybe the most expensive suite in Dallas, but then he'd decided that would put her too close to taxis or planes or other means of escape. He wanted her all to himself.

He fought all of his old past resentments—most of them, as it had turned out, unwarranted—and tracked Brian down in San Antonio, where he was practicing law. He pointed out that his former best friend owed him one for the scam he and Melissa had tried to pull on Cody years before.

"I'm just grateful that you didn't come after me with a shotgun," Brian said. "Anything you want is yours."

"Does your family still have that cabin by the lake?"

"You bet."

"Can Melissa and I borrow it for the weekend?"

"It's all yours," Brian said at once.

He told Cody where to find the key, offered some unsolicited advice on taming the reluctant Melissa, then added seriously, "I'm glad you called, buddy. I've missed you."

"Same here," Cody said. "Next time you're down this way, we'll have to get together. You do have your own woman now, don't you?"

Brian chuckled. "Do I ever. Good luck. You and Melissa should have worked this out long ago. I'd have told you the truth myself, but Melissa swore me to secrecy."

"Secrets are her specialty, it appears," Cody said. "Anyway, thanks again for the cabin."

Those arrangements made, Cody loaded groceries, flowers and nonalcoholic champagne into the back of the truck, then swung by Dolan's. He marched straight to the soda fountain, ignoring the startled gazes of the teens gathered there.

"Cody? Is everything okay?" Melissa asked as he rounded the corner of the counter and headed toward her.

"Just dandy," he confirmed, tucking one arm under her legs and the other behind her waist. He scooped her up, amid a flurry of outraged protests from her and that same pimply faced kid who'd defended her honor once before.

"It's okay, son," Cody assured him. "She wants to go with me."

"I do not!" Melissa protested.

"Eli, call the cops or something," the boy shouted, his face turning red as he bolted after Cody.

"Not on your life," Eli said, and kept right on filling prescriptions. Mabel held the door open, grinning widely.

Melissa huffed and puffed a little longer, but by the time Cody had driven to the outskirts of town, she'd retreated into a sullen silence.

"Was that caveman approach entirely necessary?" she inquired eventually.

"I thought so."

"I would have come with you, if you'd asked politely."

He shot a skeptical look in her direction.

"At least, I would have thought about it," she amended.

"That's why I didn't ask. You've been thinking entirely too much."

"Are we going to White Pines?"

"Nope."

"Luke and Jessie's?" she asked hopefully, the first little sign of alarm sparking in her eyes.

"Nope."

"Cody, where the hell are you taking me?"

"Someplace where we can be alone."

"Where?" she repeated.

"Brian's cabin."

Her eyes widened. "You talked to Brian?"

"I figured drastic measures were called for, and he promised the best and quickest solution." He glanced over at her. "I was willing to do anything it took to make this happen, sweet pea."

"Oh," she said softly, and settled back to mull that over.

It wasn't more than half an hour later when he noticed she seemed to be getting a little restless.

"You okay?" he asked.

She turned toward him, her lower lip caught between her teeth as she shook her head. Instantly, Cody's muscles tensed.

"Melissa, what's wrong?" he demanded. "Tell me."

"It's not a problem," she said. "Not yet, anyway. It's just that..." Her eyes widened and turned the color of a turbulent sea. She swallowed visibly. "Don't panic."

Cody panicked. "Melissa!"

"It's okay, really it is. It's just that it's entirely possible that I'm in labor." She sucked in a ragged breath, then announced, "Cody, I think we're about to have a baby."

Chapter Sixteen

Cody found his father already pacing the waiting room when he got Melissa to the hospital. He'd called him on his cellular phone, right after he'd spoken to the doctor. He'd asked Harlan to alert the rest of the family.

"Even Jordan?" his father had asked cautiously, aware of the friction between them.

Cody decided then and there it was time to get over the rift between him and his brother. This was a time for healing.

"Even Jordan," he'd confirmed.

He turned now to his father. "Did you reach everyone?"

"They'll be here in a bit. How is she?" Harlan demanded at once as the nurse wheeled Melissa away to prep her for delivery. "Is everything okay?"

Cody wiped a stream of sweat from his brow. "She says it is, but I don't know. You had four sons. Is labor supposed to be so painful?"

"How should I know? Your mama wouldn't let me anywhere near the delivery room. She said having babies was women's work." He glanced at Cody with an unmistakable look of envy. "Wish I'd had a chance to be there just once, though. Seems to me like it must be a flat-out miracle. You going in there with Melissa?"

"If she'll let me," Cody said. "She's still making up her mind whether to be furious at me for kidnapping her this afternoon." He moaned. "I must have been out of my mind. I didn't even think about the fact that she might go into labor."

"Cody, you weren't at the other end of the world," Harlan reassured him. "You'd barely made it out of town. You got her here in plenty of time. The only way you could have gotten here much faster would have been to park her in a room upstairs for the last month of her pregnancy. Now, settle down."

"It's easy for you. It's not your baby she's having."

Just then the nurse came out. "Mr. Adams, would you like to step in for a minute? We're getting ready to take Melissa to the delivery room."

Cody shot a helpless look at his father. "It sounds like she's not going to want me in there."

"Maybe it's time to stop bullying the girl and tell her how much you want to be there," Harlan advised.

Cody doubted it would be as simple as that. Indeed, Melissa shot him a look of pure hatred when he walked into her room. Of course, that might have had something to do with the whopper of a contraction she appeared to be in the middle of.

He accepted a damp cloth from the nurse and instinctively wiped Melissa's forehead with it.

"You're doing great," he said.

"How would you know?" she retorted.

He grinned at the fiery display of temper. "Okay, you got me. I have no idea. No one's running around the halls panicking, though. That must mean something."

"They're used to this," she retorted. "I'm not. Besides, they're just observers. I'm doing all the work."

"If you'd let me take those natural childbirth classes with you, I'd be more help about now."

She latched onto his hand just then and squeezed. It was either one hell of a contraction or she was trying to punish him by breaking all of his knuckles. As soon as the pain eased, she glared at him again.

"Go away."

"I don't think so," he countered just as stubbornly. "I want to share this with you."

"You want to see me writhing around in agony," she snapped.

"No," he insisted. "Having a baby is a miracle. I missed out on Sharon Lynn's birth. I'm going to be with you for this one."

"Why?"

He regarded her blankly. "Don't you know?"

"Cody, I don't know anything except that you've been making a pest of yourself ever since you got back into town. What I don't know is why."

Before he could answer, the orderlies came to wheel her down the hall to the delivery room. He could tell by the set of her jaw that she was going into that room without him unless he could find the courage to tell her what was in his heart.

"Dammit, Melissa, I love you!" he shouted after her, just as they were about to roll her out of sight.

"Stop!" Melissa bellowed at the orderlies between contractions.

Cody reached her side in an instant. Even with her face bathed in sweat, her lower lip bitten raw, she looked beautiful to him. She always had, always would.

"What did you say?" she demanded, then grabbed onto his hand with a grip so fierce he could have sworn that more bones broke.

He grinned through the pain—hers and his. "I said I love you."

A slow, satisfied smile spread across her face. "It's about time, cowboy."

"Haven't I been saying that for months now?" he asked, vaguely bemused that she hadn't heard it before.

"Not the words," she told him. "How was I supposed to believe it without the words?"

"Someone once told me that actions speak louder than words. I guess I was putting it to the test. I thought you needed to see that I wasn't going anywhere."

"I also needed to hear why that was so," she told him, wincing as another pain started and then rolled through her. "I didn't want you with me out of a sense of obligation."

Relief swept through him as he realized he'd risked everything and finally gotten through to her. "Does that mean you'll marry me?"

"Whenever you say."

Cody turned and motioned to the preacher he'd had Harlan call for him. He'd also had Harlan make a call to a judge to cut through the legal red tape. "Get to it, Reverend. I don't think this baby's going to wait much longer."

The minister had never talked so fast in his life, quite possibly because he was conducting the ceremony in the doorway of a delivery room. Cody figured as long as they didn't cross that threshold, the baby would have sense enough not to come until his or her parents were properly married.

The "I do's" were punctuated by moans and a couple of screams. And not five minutes later, Harlan Patrick Adams came into the world with an impeccable sense of timing, just as the minister pronounced his mama and daddy man and wife.

* * *

Melissa was beginning to wonder if she was ever going to be able to hold her own baby. Between Cody and his father, she'd barely gotten a look at him. Cody had finally disappeared a half hour before, but Harlan was still holding the baby with a look of such pride and sadness in his eyes.

"I wish Mary could have seen him," he said softly as a tear spilled down his cheek.

"Wherever she is, I think she knows," Melissa told him. "And I'll bet Erik is right beside her, watching out for all of us."

Her father-in-law gave her a watery smile. "I can't tell you how proud it makes me to have you in this family finally."

"I'm glad to be a part of it finally," she told him. "Though given the way my brand new husband scooted out of here after the ceremony, I'm not so sure I made the right decision. Any idea where he went?"

There was no mistaking the spark of pure mischief in Harlan's eyes. "Can't say that I know for sure," he said.

Melissa didn't believe him for a second. The old scoundrel and Cody were clearly up to their ornery chins in some scheme or another. Before she could try to pry their secret out of him, the door to the room slid open a crack.

"Everyone awake?" Cody inquired lightly.

"Come on in, son," Harlan enthused. "We were just wondering where you'd gone off to."

Cody stepped into the room and winked at her. "Should I take that to mean that you suspected I'd run off on you already?"

"It did cross my mind," she admitted. "You turned awful pale there in the delivery room. I figured you might be having second thoughts about marriage and fatherhood."

"Not me," Cody retorted indignantly. "I just figured the occasion deserved a celebration. You know how this family likes to party. You up for it?"

She stared at him as he watched her uneasily. "What if I say no?"

"Then that's it. I send everyone away."

"Everyone? Who is out there?"

"Sharon Lynn, first of all. She wants to meet her new baby brother."

Melissa grinned. "Bring her in. Of course I want her to see the baby."

Cody opened the door and Sharon Lynn barreled in and ran toward the bed. Over the past few months she'd grown increasingly steady on her feet. In the final weeks of her pregnancy Melissa had had a heck of a time waddling after her.

"Mama! Mama!" Sharon Lynn shouted.

Cody lifted Sharon Lynn onto the bed beside her. "Harlan, bring the baby over so Sharon Lynn can get a look," Melissa said.

As Harlan approached with the baby, her daughter's eyes grew wide. "Baby?"

"That's right, pumpkin. That's Harlan Patrick, your baby brother."

As if she knew that newborns were fragile, Sharon Lynn reached over and gently touched a finger to her brother's cheek. "I hold," she announced.

"Not yet," Melissa told her just as there was a soft knock on the door.

Cody reached for the handle, but his gaze was on her. "You ready for more visitors?"

"Who else is out there?"

"Your parents," he said.

"Luke and Jessie," Sharon Lynn chimed in, clearly proud that she'd learned two new names. "And Jordie and Kelly."

Melissa chuckled as she imagined straight-laced Jordan if he ever heard himself referred to as "Jordie." She gave her husband a warm smile, silently congratulating him for ending the feud that never should have happened.

"Let them in," she instructed Cody. "If I'd known you were inviting half the town, I'd have insisted on that private VIP suite they have upstairs."

As the family crowded in, a nurse came along, wheeling in a three-tiered wedding cake. Melissa stared at it in amazement. "When did you have time to order that?"

"Right after you said 'I do' and delivered our son," he said. "I told the bakery it was an emergency."

Kelly leaned down to kiss her cheek. "You should have seen the look on their faces when I stopped to pick it up. Obviously, they'd never heard of an emergency wedding before.''

Melissa swung her legs over the side of the bed and prepared to go over for a closer look.

"Stay right where you are," Cody ordered, looking panicked.

"I'm not an invalid," she informed him.

"It's not that," he admitted, casting a worried look at the cake. "Actually, it was a little late to come up with an emergency cake. Fortunately, they had a cancellation.''

Melissa stared at him, torn between laughing and crying. "That is someone else's cake?"

"They got the other names off," Kelly reassured her. "Almost, anyway."

Sure enough, when Melissa managed to get near enough for a closer look, she could spot the traces of blue food dye across the white icing on the top layer. Love Always had been left in place, but below it were the shadowy letters unmistakably spelling out Tom And Cecily.

Melissa grinned. "Get on over here, Tom," she said pointedly. "Give old Cecily a kiss."

Cody didn't hesitate. He gathered her close and slanted his lips across hers in a kiss that spoke of love and commitment and all the joy that was to come.

"Okay, that's enough, baby brother," Luke said. "Give the rest of us a chance to kiss the bride."

Cody relinquished his hold on her with obvious reluctance. He stood patiently by as she was kissed and
congratulated by all the others. Harlan grabbed a pa-
per cup and filled it with lukewarm water from the tap.

"A toast, everyone," he announced.

When they all had their own cups of water, he lifted
his cup. "To Cody and Melissa. This marriage was a
long time coming. There were times I despaired of the
two of you ever realizing that you belong together.
Now that you have, we wish you every happiness for all
the years to come."

"Hear, hear," Jordan and Luke echoed. "Much
happiness, baby brother."

"Now it's my turn to kiss the bride," Harlan declared, giving her a resounding smack on the cheek.

Cody stole between them. "Get your own bride, old
man. This one is mine."

"Maybe I will," Harlan said, startling them all.

Cody, Jordan and Luke stared at him in openmouthed astonishment while their wives all chuckled
with delight.

"Do it," Melissa whispered in his ear, standing on
tiptoe to give him a kiss. "Find a bride and live hap-
ily ever after. No one deserves it more. Mary would
want that for you."

She had a feeling that when Harlan Adams set his
mind to finding a woman to share his life, he was going to set all of Texas on its ear. And his sons were going to have the time of their lives getting even for all the

grief he'd given them over their own love lives. Melissa was thrilled that she was going to be right in the thick of it all, where she'd always dreamed of being.

Her mother and father came over to her then. "You happy, ladybug?" her father asked.

She clung tightly to Cody's hand and never took her gaze from his as she whispered, "Happier than I thought possible."

"About time," her mother huffed.

Cody leaned down and kissed her soundly. "Stop fussing, Velma." He grinned unrepentantly at her mother's expression of shock. "One of these days you're going to admit it," he taunted.

"Admit what?"

"That you're crazy about me."

Her mother scowled. "You're too sure of yourself, Cody Adams. Somebody's got to keep you in line."

He turned his gaze on Melissa then. "And I know just the woman to do it," he said softly.

"What if I don't want to keep you in line?" Melissa asked. "I kind of like your roguish ways."

"Told you she didn't have a lick of sense where that boy was concerned," Velma announced loudly.

Melissa glanced at her mother just then and winked. After a startled instant, her mother chuckled despite herself and winked right back. She tucked her arm through her husband's and added, "Married one just like him myself."

"Then I guess Cody and I are going to be okay, aren't we, Mother?"

Her mother glanced pointedly at Sharon Lynn and the new baby. "Looks to me like you've got quite a head start on it."

Cody brushed a kiss across her cheek. "Indeed, we do."

Everyone began leaving after that. Finally Melissa was alone with her husband. "I love you," she told him.

"I love you," he echoed. His expression turned serious. "Do you really think Daddy's going to start courting?"

"Sounded to me as if he meant what he said. How would you feel about that?"

Cody hesitated for a minute, then grinned. "Seems like a damned fine opportunity to get even with him, if you ask me."

"That's what I love about you Adams men," Melissa taunted. "You are so supportive of each other."

"You don't think he deserves to be taken on a merry chase?"

"By some woman," she admonished. "Not by you, Luke and Jordan."

He sighed and folded his arms around her middle from behind. His breath fanned across her cheek. "I suppose standing on the sidelines and watching him fall will have its moments," he agreed. "He sure seemed to get a kick out of watching that happen to the rest of us."

"Then I suggest you prepare yourself for the ride," she told him. "Knowing Harlan, it's going to be a bumpy one."

"As for you and me," Cody proclaimed, "from here on out it's going to be smooth sailing."

* * * * *

See how Harlan Adams tumbles into love with a most unlikely woman. Watch for
The Rancher and His Unexpected Daughter,
coming in March 1997
from Silhouette Special Edition.

COMING NEXT MONTH

ON MOTHER'S DAY Andrea Edwards

Great Expectations
When Alex Rhinehart reunited Fiona Scott with the daughter she'd given up for adoption, he helped her save the child she thought she'd never see again. And now that Alex and Fiona had found each other, Fiona had more than one reason to celebrate Mother's Day.

A COWBOY IS FOREVER Shirley Larson

To Luke Steadman's family, Charlotte Malone had always been from the wrong side of town. She needed his help in saving her ranch, and this time, not even feuding families would keep this cowboy from his destiny.

THE CASE OF THE BORROWED BRIDE Victoria Pade

That Special Woman!
Quinn Strummel was a hard-nosed private investigator, but he had a soft spot for damsels in distress. This one, clad in a mud-caked wedding dress and heel-less satin pumps, couldn't even remember her name! Quinn knew one thing for sure: she was trouble!

THE FATHER OF HER CHILD Joan Elliott Pickart

The Baby Bet
Ted Sharpe was carefree and single. But secretly he yearned to be a husband and a father. When the very pregnant divorcee Hannah Johnson moved in next door, he lost his heart—but found his dreams.

THE WOLF AND THE WOMAN'S TOUCH Ingrid Weaver

To find her young niece, Jenna Lawrence could turn to only one man—Damien Reese—a man living alone in a secluded mountain cabin. Jenna's sudden presence in Damien's life awakened long-buried emotions, and he agreed to help—on one condition...

THE RANCHER AND HIS UNEXPECTED DAUGHTER
Sherryl Woods

And Baby Makes Three
Harlan Adams was used to getting his way, but feisty Janet Runningbear and her daughter weren't making it easy for him. Janet sent Harlan's heart into a tailspin, until he was sure of only one thing—he wanted her as his wife!

COMING NEXT MONTH FROM

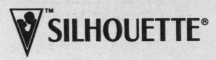
SILHOUETTE®

Intrigue
Danger, deception and desire

THE CHARMER Leona Karr
LOVE VS. ILLUSION M.J. Rodgers
BELLADONNA Jenna Ryan
MYSTERY BABY Dani Sinclair

Desire
Provocative, sensual love stories for the woman of today

YOU'RE WHAT?! Anne Eames
SURRENDER Metsy Hingle
THE TEMPORARY GROOM Joan Johnston
MICHAEL'S BABY Cathie Linz
THE BRIDE'S CHOICE Sara Orwig
REGAN'S PRIDE Diana Palmer

Sensation
A thrilling mix of passion, adventure and drama

DRIVEN TO DISTRACTION Judith Duncan
MACKENZIE'S PLEASURE Linda Howard
MICHAEL'S HOUSE Pat Warren
UNBROKEN VOWS Frances Williams

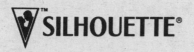

SILHOUETTE®

Treat yourself to...

Wanted:
Mother

*Silhouette's annual tribute to motherhood takes
a new twist in '97 as three sexy single men
prepare for fatherhood and saying "I Do!"*

Written by three captivating authors:

Annette Broadrick
Ginna Gray
Raye Morgan

Available: February 1997   Price: £4.99

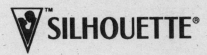
™ SILHOUETTE®

Spring is in the air with our sparkling collection
from Silhouette...

SPRING
fever

Three sexy, single men are about to find the love
of a lifetime!

Grace And The Law by Dixie Browning
Lighfoot And Loving by Cait London
Out Of The Dark by Pepper Adams

Three delightful stories...one romantic season!

Available: March 1997   Price: £4.

LAURA VAN WORMER

◇

JURY DUTY

'Dubbed the 'Poor Little Rich Boy' case,
this notorious trial will change forever the
lives of the twelve New York City
residents called to the jury.

*A legal three-ring circus with brains and
wit, populated with colorful New Yorkers of
every stripe and class*
—Kirkus Reviews

**AVAILABLE IN PAPERBACK
FROM FEBRUARY 1997**

FREE!

FOUR FREE
specially selected
Special Edition® novels
<u>PLUS</u> a Mystery Gift
when you return this card...

Return this coupon and we'll send you 4 Silhouette Special Edition® novels and a mystery gift absolutely FREE! We'll even pay the postage and packing for you.

We're making you this offer to introduce you to the benefits of the Reader Service™– FREE home delivery of brand-new Silhouette novels, at least a month before they are available in the shops, FREE gifts and a monthly Newsletter packed with information.

Accepting these FREE books and gift places you under no obligation to buy—you may cancel at any time, even after receiving just your free shipment. Simply complete the coupon below and send it to:

THE READER SERVICE, FREEPOST, CROYDON, SURREY, CR9 3WZ.

EIRE READERS PLEASE SEND COUPON TO: P.O. BOX 4546, DUBLIN 24.

NO STAMP NEEDED

Yes, please send me 4 free Special Edition novels and a mystery gift. I understand that unless you hear from me, I will receive 6 superb new titles every month for just £2.30* each, postage and packing free. I am under no obligation to purchase any books and I may cancel or suspend my subscription at any time, but the free books and gift will be mine to keep in any case. (I am over 18 years of age)

E6XE

Ms/Mrs/Miss/Mr _____
BLOCK CAPS PLEASE

Address _____

_____

_____ Postcode _____

CAROLE MORTIMER

*Their tempestuous night held a
magic all its own...and only she
could mend his shattered dreams*

Merlyn's Magic

**AVAILABLE IN PAPERBACK
FROM FEBRUARY 1997**